Cha-Ching

Charge it to the Game

A Novel by

Tonya Blount

Copyright © 2006 by Tonya Blount

Published by Two of a Kind Publishing
3120 Milton Road
Charlotte, NC 28215

www.twoofakindpublishing.com

Editor: Jermaine Vaughn & Angela Smith

Book Layout: Lisa Gibson-Wilson
            Renaissance Management Services
            www.renmanserv.com

Cover Design: Antoine Scott

First printing March 2006

Printed in the United States of America

ISBN: 0-9752589-3-1

In loving memory of Daddy:
Ronald Nathaniel Vaughn — a true warrior.
Just when I thought I could lose no more,
I lost the greatest.
What would I give to dance with my father again?
I miss you, and love you always, Daddy!

and

Tone, Mars, Britt, LaLa, and D-man
The music to my soul...

Acknowledgements

First, thanks to God for blessing me with discerning eyes to see the message through all the pain, loss, and grief.

To my beautiful children: Thank you for loving me unconditionally, for sacrificing "our" time and understanding that to whom much is given, much is required. I am so blessed! Mommy (my northern star), even in your grief, you reached out to others, you still gave your love, you still managed to smile, and you continued to give God the glory. There is no other woman in the world like you, and I am so proud that you are my mother. To my siblings: Jermaine, Ronald "Ronnie, Jr.," and Jennifer: Y'all complete my circle. I LOVE YOU!!!

I must thank the following people: James Smith, the Bradley, Baker, Wilson, Crisp, Cox, Young, Tranum, Bolling, Welcome and Woodley families, Gwendolyn Thomas, Richard "Rick" Baker, Lonnel Lewis, Tracy Matos, Angela Smith, Jeannean "Nee Nee" Ross, Yolonda Wilson, Kodzina "Koddy" Griffin (Look at God!), Chavon Thompson, Vernon Harrison, Jr., Bettie Watkins, Lonnie McKinstry, LisaRenae Johnson, and Denise Hanney.

To my writer friends for your support and love: Nathasha Brooks-Harris, C. Rene West, and Danielle Santiago. To Richmond's 106.5 The Beat's mid-day mommie, Mahogany Brown, and Marc Medley of 93.7 FM in New Jersey for your continued support.

Special thanks to Brother James Muhammad for staying on me, allowing me to join your family and share your vision. I know that I tested your patience. I hope that the final project was worth it. Your honesty is a rarity in this industry. It is so much appreciated.

I could not have created this work without my cousin, Timothy "Tim" Baker. Thank you for assisting me with the research and most of all your support and ear no matter what hour of the day I called. This is it…for real, boo!

Love and blessings to the courageous sisters whom I have been blessed to meet during my visits at domestic violence shelters, I know first hand your plight; remember that God is a deliverer. To my brothers on lock down (especially Todd, Jay, and Andre) your letters have touched my life, too. Hugs to my loyal readers and fans, you continue to inspire me with your emails.

Laboring and giving birth to this project was the most challenging yet. In less than five months, I suddenly lost three significant people in my life. Writing, the natural process that usually heals my soul was impossible to do. The words danced in my head, the characters spoke, but my heart was broken and I lost the passion to create. With that said, I give honor to the following people that have went on to Glory for allowing their spirits to comfort me when I needed them the most: To a true Queen...Akua Pace: Thank you for being the sister that my mother needed. You were the epitome of what a woman should be. The world is missing your beautiful spirit. Jeffrey "Jay" Lewis (my hero): Recently, I had to mourn you all over again and it hurt just like the very first time. Fly free and in peace, Crystal Bowers: you have earned your wings. And to my Daddy: The handsome, brave and talented man that shook things up on this earth. I know you are watching and protecting me, I feel your spirit when I need you the most. Still, I would do anything to have you sitting next to me right now. I hope you know how proud I was of you...I still am. Love you, Ton.

Peace and blessings,

Tonya Blount
tonyablount@yahoo.com

The streets don't got no soul…so I trust no bitch!
Storm Williams

Prologue

"Why do you care so much?" I shouted. "Why do you care why I have chosen this life? I mean you keep talking about what made me choose this path...what made me take this road? What makes you think I chose *it*? How do you know that *it* didn't choose me?"

"You're right. I don't know," the interviewer responded. "Why don't you tell me?"

"You got to know where I've been to know who I am," I replied in a voice filled with rage. "Why the hell do you care?"

"I care because I am a woman of God," the interviewer replied. "The word says, the Lord asks how can you love me and you have never seen me and not love your neighbor. So--"

"Didn't I tell you before I don't want to hear that shit?"

I interrupted. "I ain't tryin' to hear that. If that's all you got to talk about then you can get the hell out of here. I don't need to hear that shit right now. It ain't gonna help me."

"Okay, then what do you think will help you?"

"What's gonna help me? What's gonna help me is getting out of here...this hospital bed and make me better, so I can go home. Tell *your* God to do that. Can He do that?" Suddenly a thick cloud of bitterness filled the air.

"Yes, He can," she answered softly.

I turned my head away. "Uh, huh...I bet."

"Why are you so bitter and angry with the Lord? What happened to you?"

"Oh, so now what...*you* can't see?"

"This...your anger, and your bitterness transcends beyond why you are here now. It's deeper than this moment."

My lips began to twitch. *How could she know?* "It don't matter."

"Yes, it does. Please tell me what happened to you."

"Why should I?" I snapped. "I don't know you. Tell me why the fuck should I trust you?"

"Because somewhere deep inside...you want to let it go," the interviewer answered patiently. "I know you do. You want to let go of the pain that has held you in captivity. You need to free yourself," the interviewer took my hand. "You need to speak to the Lord and tell Him why you're angry."

I turned my head to face her and mumbled, "Ain't shit to say."

"I don't believe that. In fact, I think the opposite. I believe you have a lot you want to say."

CHA-CHING

"I don't give a damn what you believe!"

"Storm, you can lay there and cuss, and be mean all you want...I'm not going anywhere today until you tell me. You are not going to scare me away." She gently took my hand and placed it in hers. "So you might as well start talking. Go on...tell me what happened the day you believe that God stopped hearing you."

That last sentence had quickly opened up the floodgate of my memory, the painful memory attached to a past I had tried to forget -- one that had scarred me the last 14 years of my life. That tragic day that marked the beginning of it. In an instant, I was eleven years old again. I carefully licked my lips, took a deep breath and finally shared my history.

Part I

Why *it* chose me?

Chapter 1

May 1989

I hated Thursday nights. No matter what I did I wasn't ever able to convince Aunt Hope to take me along with her to Bingo. She knew I couldn't stand her stink-lazy-ass-dope fiend countrified boyfriend Smoke, but she acted like she didn't care and she would leave me with him anyway.

While Aunt Hope was gone I would usually try and keep myself occupied writing in my diary. I had been writing in it since I was six years old. Sometimes when I write in my diary I think of Momma, and then I get real sad. That was the only present under the tree for me in Christmas of 1984. In fact, that was the last thing my Momma gave me. Momma went to the store right after I opened up my gift, and she never came back. After the second day had passed by, and all the Ritz crackers were gone, my stomach was hurting real bad…it felt like an 18 wheeler truck had landed in there and broke down. I started vomiting all over the place. But no food came out—just some bubbly yellowish spit. I remember I was so scared. I thought I was gonna die right then and there.

I crawled out of the living room window and went down the fire escape to Miss Penny's house. She never locked her window. I think because she knew I came and ate some of her food once in a while. She never caught me, I was always careful and I would make sure to clean up my mess. But I could tell she knew I was there by the way she would look at me sometimes when we would pass each other in the hallway. She would give me that I-know-you-snuck-in-my-house-but-I-ain't-gonna-tell-cause-I-fell-sorry-for-you look.

When I got inside of Miss Penny's house, I went in the kitchen, took a Twinkie and then I called Aunt Hope. About an hour later she came and got me. Now Aunt Hope wasn't really my aunt, she was my Momma's best friend, but she always acted like my aunt.

When I was too sad to write, I would start to crochet. I loved to crochet. Aunt Hope taught me how to do it. I used to like to make new things. But we didn't have a lot of money, so sometimes I had to take a loose some of the things I had made just so I could make something else. I hated it when I had to do that.

This night…I felt too sad to write, and too mad to crochet. So I decided to turn on the T.V. and started watching *Knots Landing*—one of my favorite shows. Now, I loved watching how rich white people lived. And I promised myself that one day I was gonna live just like them. I had it all planned out. By the time, I was 16, I was gonna pack up all of my diaries, Ashley—my baby doll, my crochet needle and I was gonna leave tired ass Bushwick and move to Manhattan where all the rich people lived. And I wasn't never ever gonna look back. Well, I thought about calling Aunt Hope once in a while—just to see if she heard from my Momma. But that was it.

I always dreamt big. I was gonna live in a tall building, right next to the Empire State Building, with a doorman, a red sports car—maybe a Honda Accord, twenty pairs of high heeled shoes, different panties for every day of the week, and a cute husband—with a lot of money. And he had to have a lot of his *own* money. I had watched Aunt Hope take care of dope fiend Smoke and I knew I wasn't hardly 'bout to take care of no man.

Smoke always had a house full of company when Aunt Hope would leave the house. And all his friends were dope fiends just like him. The only good thing about them coming over was it would keep Smoke out my face while they were there. He was always ordering me around like he was my father.

This night was a little different…there was a man I had never seen before. He was high-yellow with ringlets of curly brown hair, freckles and green eyes--they were a little darker than mine. He didn't look so poor either. I didn't know what he was doing hanging out with those dope fiends though. I thought maybe he didn't know they were. On second thought, he had to know because they had been in there really cutting up…laughing, coughing and then laughing again. When they did that that always meant they were getting high.

I tried not to pay them no attention and kept on watching *Knots Landing*--even though it was a repeat. But all of the sudden it got real quiet. No laughing or coughing. Nothing. I thought I heard a little whispering but that was it. I turned down the volume on the T.V. to see if I could hear anything but I didn't. So, I tipped-toed all the way to the end of the hallway and peeped through the beads that were hanging from the archway, and I couldn't believe my eyes. Smoke was sitting on the couch holding this glass pipe with smoke coming out of it and was tongue kissing Skeet. Bill was taking his hand and was slowly going up and down on the high-yellow man's dick. Then he stuck his tongue out and started licking the pink part—just like he was licking ice cream. Then the high-yellow man pushed Bill's head toward his dick and Bill put the *whole* thing in his mouth. The whole thing. All I saw was his hair. It wasn't pretty and curly like the hair on his head either. The hair that was wrapped around his dick was black and looked nappy.

The horrific scene made a sudden queasiness ripple in my stomach. The dinner that I had eaten earlier was trying to make an exit. I was trying to keep it in but started to gag. I ain't mean to make any noise, it just came out. Smoke heard me and he quickly took his tongue out of Skeets' mouth, pushed him away and looked at me. I panicked and tried to run, but my eyes had already connected with Smoke's and the hate in his bloody red eyes had paralyzed me. Finally, he nodded to Skeet and whispered, "Oh, shit, Storm." His words were magical because in a quickness they moved both of my feet and I ran as fast as I could right back into my room.

CHA-CHING

I sat on the radiator staring at the darkness of the alleyway wondering what I should do. Then, footsteps interrupted my thoughts. I started to count each one as they walked pass my bedroom and exited the apartment. Suddenly, I heard Smoke walking then he stopped at my doorway. Everything felt as if it were going in slow motion. My heart started beating so fast. I knew Smoke was gonna spank the living shit out of me for snooping around. Aunt Hope had always told me I was too nosey for my own good and I needed to stay out of grown folks business. Did I listen? No, me and my nosey ass self had to go searching for trouble. And I wasn't happy until I saw Smoke and his friends fucking.

All I could think to do was put on layers of clothing, in an attempt to minimize the pain. I grabbed my corduroy pants and put them on, then my Michael Jordan hooded sweatshirt. I looked around my room hoping an escape would miraculously appear. Nothing.

Finally, the door opened and I saw Smoke's shadow and I quickly felt his anger. I cleared my thought. "I'm... I'm sorry," I stammered while pushing the dangling strands of hair away from my face. "I'm sorry Smoke. I ain't mean to be minding your business. I was hungry and I just wanted to go...I mean I was getting--"

Smoke slowly shut and locked the door. Then he walked over to me, covered my mouth and stared down at me with a curious look. For some reason, I began to feel ashamed...knowing what I had witnessed. I looked away, avoiding eye contact. *Aunt Hope, please come home.* Aunt Hope wasn't expected home for another forty-five minutes, and time didn't show any mercy, it continued crawling on broken legs.

"Take off your clothes, Storm," Smoke demanded in a southern drawl.

"Why?" I asked wiping away the warm tears off of my cheeks. Then I started backing away from him, using my hands to guide me around the tiny dark room. I hoped I would get lucky and talk him out of it. "I said I'm sorry Smoke. I ain't gonna tell...I promise you. You got my word, I ain't gonna say nothing. Just forget I saw you. Okay? That's all. All right, Smoke?"

In a flash, Smoke reached, grabbed me by my sweatshirt and threw me on my bed. The sounds of the mattress springs echoed off the quiet walls. "I ain't gonna tell your ass again. Take off your fuckin' clothes or I'm gonna take them off *for* you."

"Don't spank me," I pleaded. Suddenly the look in his eyes told me I was about to get more than a spanking. "Pleeaaaaase, Smoke. No."

Smoke started ripping my pants off. I struggled and wiggled to get away from him. But I couldn't beat his quickness or strength. He pulled me back toward him. With one hand he covered my mouth, and the other hand he unzipped his pants. Then an awful smell of musk and funk was immediately released. I started to gag. But I had no time to get ill, I had to stop Smoke. I punched him in his back, and dug my nails in his skin. Then with all of my strength I pushed down on his shoulder blades. All of my attempts to free myself from his vicious hold were futile.

Please God stop him. I thought as I moved my head from side-to-side. *Please God don't let him put that thing in me.*

"If you promise to be quiet I'll let you go. I'm just gonna show you something. I ain't gonna hurt you. Okay? You promise you'll be quiet?"

I nervously shook my head yes.

Smoke moved his stiff member closer to my private. "Now, I'm telling you...if you scream, I'ma put it in. I'm 'bout to take my hand off. If you say one fuckin' word, I'm gonna push it in. You ready?"

"Umm hmm."

Smoke lifted his fingers, one by one. Then he lifted his palm off of my lips. I wanted to scream for help. However, the thickness and the heat penetrating from his penis reminded me of his earlier warning. I decided against it.

"Why you doin' this to me?" I cried. Even at my young age, I always knew that Smoke was in moral prison, yet I never could have imagined him doing this to me.

Without saying a word, Smoke smacked me. My face was stinging then it became numb. "Didn't I tell you not to open up your mouth? You such a gotdamn actress! You don't' listen...do you? Huh? That's your damn problem...so hardheaded. Now see what you done made me do."

I knew I had nothing else to lose. No matter whether I was quiet or not, Smoke was going to rape me. I pleaded with him once more. "Why? But I'm a little girl." I reminded him in a whisper.

Smoke ignored me. He grabbed my hands and without warning or pity he furiously rammed himself in my frail body. My entire body was burning in pain. I don't know how, but Smoke was enjoying it.

"God, pleeeeeze make him stop! Make him stop!" Fear and anger had begun to collide.

"Don't you know God don't owe you nothin', honey," Smoke angrily retorted.

Despite my pleas, God didn't intervene. Before Momma had slid into darkness, she would take me to church. I use to love to go because I loved the singing, and I loved seeing everybody so happy. I remember Momma would get so happy she would dance and shout all over the church and talk in a different language. One time I asked her what she was doing and she said that when she did that she was slain in the Spirit and talking to the Lord. Then it occurred to me why God hadn't stopped Smoke yet. He couldn't hear me. So I started talking like Momma did when she spoke to God. But He didn't hear that either because the more I spoke, the harder Smoke pounded on my raw and dry pussy.

Chapter 2

Smoke didn't take everything from me that night. I still managed to own a tiny piece of joy. Sometimes I had to dig deep to find it.

Although Smoke wore the evidence that proved he had violated me, Aunt Hope still refused to believe it. She couldn't face what Smoke did to me because accepting it would mean that her man wasn't who she thought he was. Instead of confronting the obvious she ignored it and she worked even harder to please Smoke. She cooked, cleaned, worked, even ironed his draws and jumped whenever he coughed.

No matter how many times Aunt Hope changed her hair dos, how much weight so lost on Weight Watchers, the Bahamian Diet or Slim Fast, or how good she cooked or screwed Smoke, he was still the same sorry ass loser and her conscious wouldn't let her forget or ignore the truth. For almost two years, she was in a constant battle of denying or accepting. Eventually, denying it ate her away and left her with a crumbled and decaying soul.

"Storm," Aunt Hope yelled from the kitchen. "Didn't I tell you to clean up the damn kitchen?"

"I'm coming," I answered sleepily. "Gimme five minutes."

"Five minutes? No. Bring your ass here right now...right this second, Storm! I'm tired of repeating myself over and over again with you."

I sucked my teeth and released a heavy sigh. "But I'm tired."

"And don't be in there talkin' under your breath either. Don't let me have to come in there and smack the shit out of your ass."

What she got bionic ears now? "I ain't say nothing," I answered back.

"Just get your ass in here and clean this kitchen!"

I got up from the bed and put my slippers on. *I gotta make a move soon*, I thought.

* * *

"You can throw them pots and pans around all you want but you betta not break a fuckin' thing or it's gonna me and you tonight."

"It's me and you every night," I mumbled.

Aunt Hope put her crack pipe down; got up from the sofa and walked into the kitchen. "What you just say?"

"Nothing," I answered back nervously.

"No, bitch," Aunt Hope began ramming her index finger on my temple. You said something...I'm tired of your ass thinking you grown. There is only one queen in this fuckin' palace and that's me! You think you so bad then you know what you can do...you can get the hell out my fuckin' house. That's what!"

I had grown tired of the daily threats and tired of screwing nasty old men to support her and Smoke's crack habit but it wasn't time to leave yet. I was only thirteen years old and fucking for free. I had to plan.

"I'm sorry," I lied hesitantly. It wasn't because I didn't know how to lie. It was what followed after it.

"You damn right you sorry...a sorry lazy ass. That's what you are. No wonder Lisa left you. You drove the poor woman crazy. She was fine before she had you. Your momma was beautiful *and* smart ass shit. Yes she was. I mean how many black woman morticians you know? None. That's how many. She was all of that...a good Christian woman with a beautiful future ahead of her. 'Til she met your sorry ass father and that was all she wrote. She got knocked up with you and when you was born all you did was cry. Tank had to feed her drugs to keep the poor woman from goin' crazy.

"You cried for two years straight. You know that? I ain't never seen a baby like you in my life...cry, cry, cry. That's all you did." Aunt Hope walked back into the living room and sat on the sofa. She had told me this story more times than I could remember. Yet every time Aunt Hope told it, the words spoke to my heart as if it were the very first time. Every since I told her that Smoke had raped me, Aunt Hope became a stranger to me. Smoke acted like a bitch, and I was the enemy to them both.

Aunt Hope took the plastic bag off of her hair and unbuttoned her jeans. "Smoke did I ever tell you, Storm cried so much I wouldn't even shake a man's *hand*...too scared I would get pregnant and end up having a child like Storm. You know that's why I ain't never have no kids...because of Storm." They both laughed. Aunt Hope picked up the lighter and began smoking.

The phone began to ring.

"Storm answer the phone! I don't understand why you gotta let it ring four or five times before you pick it up anyway. Any other kid would be happy and running to answer the phone."

"Hello. Yes, hold on." My palms instantly became sweaty. Rells was a drug kingpin. When Aunt Hope and Smoke ran up their tab and didn't have the money to pay it off they offered Rells free reign of my body. I turned my attention to Aunt Hope. "It's Rells."

"Rells?" Aunt Hope asked.

"Yes," I answered handing her the telephone.

Aunt Hope covered the mouthpiece and whispered. "You know what he probably calling for...so go on and get yourself ready. 'Cause I ain't got no money."

"But...but, I'm tired and I got a test tomorrow."

"No buts," she snapped. "Hand me that phone and go on and get out my face."

* * *

CHA-CHING

I knew it was time to plan my escape from hell. The flicker of joy I had managed to keep had allowed me to continue daydreaming about one day being a famous singer...the next Monica. The longer I stayed there, the longer it would take me to become a star.

There was one thing that Smoke, Bill, Dollar Bill, Mousie, Rells and the rest of the men I was forced to have sex with had in common...they never looked me in the eye. Deep down inside they were just like the boys my age...insecure but always trying to act powerful. They enjoyed my fear. The more I cried, the harder they would hump on me. If there was anything I had learned lately from Aunt Hope was she knew how to make you feel ashamed and powerless. If I tried to stand up for myself, she would bring me right down with her hurtful words and attack on Momma.

I had a plan, this time when Rells humped on me, I humped back. He stopped immediately. Then he slighted lifted himself off of me and looked me in the eyes. I put my hands on his butt, pulled him back toward me, and slowly moved again...this time I moaned. With everything in me, I pretended to enjoy the thickness of the unwanted flesh that was inside of me. Then I tightly closed my eyes and fantasized about LL Cool J. I opened my legs as wide as I could, then I began to sing his name, "Rellllls." Without saying a word, Rells abruptly withdrew his shriveled penis out of me; pulled up his draws, and then his sweatpants. When Rells reached the door; he dug in his pocket took something out and threw it on top of the milk crate.

TONYA BLOUNT

I got up; picked up the crisped $50 dollar bill and smiled. I had messed up his head and *finally* got paid.

Chapter 3

Winter hung around longer than it should have. It was April 1st and three inches of snow had fallen on the city during the night.

The good thing about the winter time was it was easy to hide stolen goods. I could easily stuff a coat inside *my* coat if I wanted to. Selling coats and clothes always brought me quick cash. However, with spring around the corner, I knew I had to come up with another way to stash clothes.

After my initiation with Rells, I realized there was money to be made selling my goodies. In order to look the part, I had to have the clothes and the cosmetics. I started with helping myself to Revlon's make up, and Exclamation perfume at Duane Reade's. I would use my bus pass and take the B52 to downtown Brooklyn and go shopping. I would always make sure to leave with a paid item -- even if it were only a pack of Big Red chewing gum.

To my surprise, boosting was easy and I never got caught. By the time, I was fourteen I started "shopping" in Sears, then I graduated to Macy's. Observation was the best teacher. I would browse around the store until I found a seasoned booster. Then I would watch them go behind the racks, out of the view of the big black ball. There they would bite the alarms off. I tried it and got it right the very first time.

It was important that I looked the part in whatever role I was in. Whether it was to sell the goods or wear the goods that I stole. I was driven and acted the part well.

Money was my sole motivation, because having it was the only way I could escape the two occupants that ran fiery hell on Putnam Street -- Aunt Hope and Smoke. Every dollar I earned, I secretly kept from Aunt Hope and saved for my emancipation. I made a vow to myself that by the time I was seventeen, I would be gone from there and living on my own.

* * *

Exiting the back of the bus, I noticed Looney Tootie sitting inside the bus shelter. Looney Tootie was an elderly homeless woman known by the entire neighborhood. She was given the name "Looney" because you would often see her talking and screaming at the air. I never thought anything was wrong with her because a lot of what she said made sense. She was actually the only person in the world that I had learned something positive from. Looney Tootie always told me as long as I had my mind I was free.

Looney Tootie was carefully guarding a large Conway bag and two small Pathmark bags which contained everything that she owned. For once, she was dressed appropriately for the weather. She had layers and layers of clothing on – two coats, a multi colored crocheted hat and red worn holey gloves. It didn't matter what the season was, Looney Tootie dressed the same. I often wondered what kept her from passing out during some of New York City's heat wave.

"Hi, Miss LT," I said.

Slowly lifting her head up from her chest Looney Tootie, replied, "heeeey sugggga. How you?"

"I'm good."

"Whatcha got good in dat bag?"

"Just a pair of pants."

"You ain't got no food."

"Nah. You hungry?"

"Yeah, I'm hungry."

I reached in my pocket and pulled out a single $20 bill. "This is all I got on me. Come on and walk with me around the corner to Popi's so I can get some change."

"Oh, you want me to go wit' you to Popi's?"

"Yes. Come on," I said beckoning her in my direction.

"We gonna go to Popi's so he can make us some change?"

I huffed. "Yes, Miss LT. Now come on I gotta get home. You know how Aunt Hope be acting."

Looney Tootie kicked the empty 40 ounce bottle of Colt 45 out of her way and quickly stuffed her bags under the wooden bench in the shelter. Turning her attention to me, she said, "Oh, you gotta hurry home to Hope and the devil."

"Yes," I replied with a laugh.

"You know they 'bout to be whipped. And when they do they gonna go straight to hell."

"I know. You always tell me that."

"I mean it this time, baby. You gotta pay attention to the signs, chile'. It ain't snowing in April for nothin'. God is sending the snow to cleanse the earth. Demons 'bout to fleeeeee. You hear what I tell you."

"Please Miss LT, I ain't in no mood to hear about that warfare stuff today."

"Alright, alright. I know. Storm, you ain't never in the mood 'cause you don't like all that God and demon talk. But you watch what I tell you, them demons 'bout to flee! But don't you tell nobody what ol' Tootie tell you. You keep quiet. Here?"

"I won't tell nobody what you say Miss LT. You know I never do."

"You know why you can't right?"

"Uh huh."

"A closed mouth catch no flies but loose lips sink ships," we said in unison.

As we turned onto Marcus Garvey Boulevard, I quickly noticed Smoke walking toward the telephone booth in front of Popi's bodega. It was always easy to spot Smoke. He was slightly hunchbacked and swung his hands from left to right when he walked. Smoke was with another crack head named Snoppy. I quickly turned around, hoping to get around the corner and hide behind the dumpster. I wanted to avoid the usual spectacle that occurred when Smoke or Aunt Hope caught me in the street.

"Storm!" Smoke yelled.

I pretended I didn't hear him and continued to walk while simultaneously lifting the shopping bag in my arms and trying to stuff it inside of my coat. I had about five steps to go until I reached the dumpster. If I made it there I would hide.

"STORRRRM," Smoke's voice grew closer and louder. "You hear me calling you. You besta turn 'round and get your ass back here...right now! I ain't gonna call your ass again."

I stopped my tread, slowly turned around and let out a heavy sigh. "Huh?"

"What the fuck you mean, huh? Who you think you talking to? Where the hell you think you're going?"

"I just--," I had started to say.

Smoke had reached me and looked down at me with his intimidating eyes. "Hope been looking all over for you. Why you so late getting home from school?"

"I had to stop at my friend's house and pick up something."

"What?"

"I said I had to go to my friend's house and pick up something."

"I heard that dumb ass. What did you have to pick up?"

"Something."

"Don't play with me Storm. I ain't gonna ask you again."

"My shirt."

"Your shirt?"

"Yeah."

"What the hell is your shirt doing at somebody's house?"

"I let her borrowed it."

"Her? Whose her?"

I nervously shifted from side to side and huffed. "Umm...Nee Nee."

"Who the hell is a Nee Nee? You don't know nobody name Nee Nee."

"Yes, I do. How you gonna tell me I don't know her?"

"Bitch, you done bumped your damn head!" Then Smoke smacked me on the side of my head. "Who the fuck do you think you talking to?"

Tears quickly escaped my eyes. I was enraged. I had been humiliated too many times by him and Aunt Hope. I looked over to my left and Miss LT was still standing in the same position. She nodded at me, reminding me that I needed to answer the question.

I nearly choked on the lump that sat in my throat. "Sorry. She goes to my school...that's why you don't know her." I stammered.

"You a damn liar!" Smoke said as he grabbed my coat and pulled me. "You lie so damn much you believe your own gotdamn lies."

Looney Tootie broke her silence. "You oughta be shame of yourself...treating that chile' like that!"

"Mind you gotdamn business! Who you think you are? Telling me what to do with my child? What you need to be worrying about is finding some where to wash your ass. That's what you need to be doing...crazy bitch!"

"I ain't your child," I mumbled while moving my head from side to side.

"You take care of yourself now, sugar," Looney Tootie warned.

Releasing myself from Smoke's hold, I replied, "I will, Miss LT."

When I reached where Miss LT stood, I grabbed her by the hand and quickly placed the $20 bill in it. "Here's your dollar back."

Looney Tootie paused for a moment. "You sure, sugar?"

"What the hell is going on?" Smoke snapped.

I started to walk away. "Nothing. Just giving back Miss LT her dollar."

Luckily Big John had turned the corner because I didn't know what lie I could make up next.

"Hey, man, what's going on?" Big John asked. Then the two gave each other a high five. I don't know why he still held onto the name Big John though. Smoking that crack had shriveled him to droopy skin and bones. Even Michael Jackson frail ass was bigger than him.

"Ain't nothing man. Just working hard...you know."

Yeah, right. Where at? Smoking your brains out at the crack den. I thought.

Then Big John looked at me. "Hey, Storm. I tell you...the older you get the more you look like Lisa. She spit you right out."

"Hi," I answered dryly.

"She mean and crazy like her, too." Smoke added.

"How's your old lady?" Big John asked folding his arms.

"She doing good. Everybody fine. How 'bout your family?"

"Oh, everybody doing alright. Yeah, yeah everybody doing good."

"What came out?"

"769."

"769?! Ain't that some shit. That came out 'bout a week ago. Didn't it?"

"Uh, huh. Played Tuesday 'fore last."

"I'm looking for those triple two's man."

"Yeah. It's about time for them to come out."

Then Smoke took a few steps closer to Big John. "So, uh, you know um…what you got good?"

Bingo! Those were the key words. Aunt Hope would be lucky if she saw Smoke within three days.

"Got a little something," Big John muttered.

"Storm you go on home. Tell Hope I'll be home in a few minutes." Smoke then handed me a small brown bag. "Here, give this to her. Its some loosies…and a beer. Make sure you give it to her…and take your ass straight home. Don't get lost, here."

"Okay, okay." *I hate his guts. I wish his crack head ass would get run over by a truck.*

"I see you later, Storm," Looney Tootie said.

"See you later, Miss LT."

"Take care of yourself."

"I will."

"See you later. Bye, sugar."

"Alright go on, Miss LT."

"Oh, Storm," Looney Tootie called out.

I turned around to face her, "What Miss LT? What you want? You heard what he said...I gotta hurry up and go on home."

"Don't you ever forget what I told you...the weakest people come to the strongest with the weakest bullshit!"

* * *

"Storm, that's you?" Aunt Hope called out.

"Yeah, it's me."

"Where the fuck you been?" Aunt Hope full lips was twisted to the side indicating she had recently gotten high. "I done sent the army out there looking for you!"

I handed her the brown bag and sat silently on the sofa.

"You hear me? I ain't gonna ask you again either?"

"I went to my friend's house and then I ran into Smoke."

"You ain't been with Smoke no damn four hours I know."

"I told *you* I was at my friend house. I went there first."

"Oh, really. Who died and left you in charge?"

"Ain't nobody."

"You damn right. I done told your ass over and over again, you ain't grown." Aunt Hope began stumping her feet. "This here is my palace. And I'm the queen of this bitch. You don't run this show. I runs this show. You do what I tell you to do. And I told you to bring your ass straight home from school.

"I take a whole lot of shit from your triflin' spoiled ass. But what I'm *not* gonna take is your ass fucking with my money. 'Cause I got bills to pay 'round here and I gotta put food on the table. And you fucking with my money, Storm. And nobody and

I mean noooooobodeeee...fucks with Hope Davis' money. You got that?"

"What you mean I'm messing with your money?"

"You know exactly what I mean! Don't you play dumb with me!"

"Why do I have to keep doing that? I don't wanna do it anymore."

"Can you take care of yourself?"

"No...not yet. But—"

"But shit! Until your ass is grown and can take care of yourself you ain't got no say so in this. You ain't gotta pot to piss in, nor a window to throw it outta...but you think you can sit here and tell me what you don't want to do and what you want to do. I ain't working and until I could find some decent work you gonna have to keep fucking. I'm doing it...what makes you think you too good to do it?"

Doing it with who? Who the hell wants your crack head ass? I thought. "I ain't say I was too good. I mean...I'm only fourteen years old."

"I don't give a gotdamn!" Aunt Hope walked toward the kitchen. "And I'm done talkin' about it. You betta go on and get yourself ready...'cause Rells been calling here and I ain't got shit to give him...but you."

"How he calling here? We ain't got no phone no more. Did you forget that?"

"I meant to say, he been *by* here. And don't you try and be smart. You betta take your smart ass in that bathroom and get that funky pussy ready. That's what."

"I got my period."

"Well, if you know like I do...you betta get ready and suck on his dick like you do those cherry blow pops. Now go on and get out of my face! I'm done talking 'bout this shit."

Recently, I had watched this talk show – I think it was Sally Jesse Raphael. There was a man on there being interviewed and I never forgot what he said, "50-50 is a partnership, but 90-10 is employment." Instantly I thought to myself, *what was 100 – 0?* I stood up, walked over to Aunt Hope ready to offer my proposition. "Okay, I'll do it. But you gotta give me $10 every time I fuck for your habit."

"Pay you?" Aunt Hope asked and then fell over laughing. "Pay YOU? Bitch, you betta be glad you got somewhere to lay your gotdamn head every night." My confrontation had obviously made her nervous. She paused for a second to light her cigarette. "You musta fell and hit your head *ten* times! Asking me for some damn money." Aunt Hope continued and dramatically began moving her head from side-to-side. She reminded me of someone my age. Then she stood up, looked down on me with her vengeful eyes and concluded, "Don't you ever *ever* in your pathetic ass life ask me again 'bout some damn money! You here me?"

Fed up with her trifling ways, I pointed to my treasure and angrily retorted, "Bitch, this pussy ain't free and this body ain't gonna be a slave for you or your sorry ass nigga no more!" Leaving her stone still from my response, I walked away, went into my room and put my diary; Exclamation perfume; make up bag; crochet needle and some panties in a Key Food plastic bag -- and left. I didn't know where I was heading to but I knew I had to get out of that hell.   No, that couldn't be hell, because even hell had to be better than there.

* * *

When I walked out the building Miss LT was standing in front of the door.   She was practically hyperventilating, yelling and swinging aimlessly at the air.   When Miss LT spotted me she quickly stopped.   Gasping for her breath, she walked up to me. "Storm, sugar, I'm so glad to see you."

"What you doing here Miss LT?   I told you to go on back to the bus stop."

"I know...I know, Storm," Looney Tootie stammered. "Buta ra' but...but I heard from God see.   And...and I had to come and tell you."

I was angry with the world at that moment.   The last thing I needed to hear was Looney Tootie preaching to me.   "Miss LT, I don't mean no harm, but I really don't feel like hearing that dumb shit right now.   I ain't tryin' to take away what you believe and everything.   But I'm telling you your God don't live there.   He can't be."

"Oooo, chile'!   Who you think you talking to...using that kinda language?   You besta go on and wash your mouth out with some soap.   And my God is your God and He is everywhere."

"I'm sorry, Miss LT.   I ain't mean to disrespect you.   I just got into a fight with Aunt Hope."

"I know.   I told you I heard from God."

"I gotta go Miss LT.   I can't be standing in front of this door 'cause Aunt Hope might come downstairs.   And I'm telling you the way I feel right now…I'ma hurt her if she come with some stupid shit."

Looney Tootie ignored my foul language this time. "Storm, you gonna be alright."

"I know."

"Look chile'." Looney Tootie looked up and pointed to my window. There were two birds circling around the window. Suddenly, one of the birds stopped circling and began pecking at the glass. I looked at Miss LT – waiting for an explanation. However, she said nothing. Instead, she wore a face I had never seen before. It wasn't fear though. I can't say what it was, but her reaction scared me.

"What's going on? What you want me to look at?"

"You see them birds?"

"Yes, I see 'em."

"You see them birds?" Looney Tootie repeated. "They trying to get in. That's what they trying to do."

"What you talking about? Birds don't wanna go inside nobody house, Miss LT. Birds like to be free. They can't be free to fly if they in a house."

"Oh, sugar but they do wanna go in. They gotta go in. See when the birds go inside of a house, they 'bout to let the death angel in."

"What?"

Looney Tootie bent down and whispered. "Death is coming, Storm."

"Miss LT, why you trying to scare me like that?"

"Death is on the way."

"MISS LT!" I screamed. "Stop that!"

"I can't stop it, Storm."

"Yes, you can. Stop talking like that."

"Storm, now you know ol' Tootie don't lie. I ain't never lied to you. And I ain't 'bout to start lying to you either. Don't be scared, sugar. I promised you the day was gonna come. Didn't I? And when it does, they both goin' straight to hell with gasoline draws on."

* * *

The next morning, Smoke jumped out of the living room window and killed himself. The word on the street was he got a hold of some bad drugs. Before he jumped, he yelled out to Aunt Hope – "Look at me, I'm Superman!"

My only regret…I wish I had been there to see him fly.

Part II

Things done changed...

Chapter 4

I knew that in order to survive, I had to continue to sell what drove old men crazy and kept them coming back for more. I had mastered wrapping my walls around their penises like no other woman before me and I enjoyed every minute of it. Not the sex – the power and control. Making grown men -- 20, 30, sometimes 40 years older than me, cry like a newborn baby was an adrenaline rush of infinite power.

I still had no place to call home. Therefore, I slept wherever I grew tired. Sometimes it would be an abandoned building, sometimes I would get one of my Johns to pay for a night at the motel, or sometimes I would sleep at Nee Nee's house. When I was really desperate, I slept wherever Miss LT did.

Everything I owned, I carried in my blue Jansport back pack. I stopped going to school and I taught myself better than any teacher could have.

I never complained, because all in all living on the streets was still better than with Aunt Hope. Besides, there was a part of me that enjoyed the adventure and the spontaneity of my lifestyle.

Aunt Hope contacted me one time after I left. She had put the word on the street that she had heard from my mother. That was the only way I would go looking for her. Aunt Hope was only able to tell me that Momma was doing fed time for being a mule, and that she was locked up somewhere in West Virginia.

For the first time since my mother had left me, I didn't feel the urgency or the desire to go searching for her. I felt some relief that she was still alive. However, somewhere along my travels, I had grown to despise her. I finally accepted what Aunt Hope and Smoke unfortunately wouldn't let me forget – she had abandoned her responsibility to me and because of that, I had already done hard core street time. Fed time was easy street. *She's doing better than me.* I reasoned.

By the time I was seventeen, I was ready to find another way to survive. I got bored with the danger, trite of the strange dicks and fed up with the sorry stories that came along with the empty sex. I did everything to my Johns that their wives or women wouldn't, I fucked, sucked and unwillingly became an unqualified therapist.

Finally, I walked away from that hustle and went from hoeing myself for $50 a night to making $5,000 a day boosting. I graduated at the top of my class and without looking back, rose to the top -- catering to the big ballers, pimps and drug dealers. I

CHA-CHING

stole and sold everything from televisions and diamonds to fur coats. While shopping in Saks one day, I met Pam -- my right hand chick who introduced me to my first connect in the credit card game. After that, it was a wrap.

Chapter 5

November 2003

I had lived in practically every borough in New York City, and in every imaginable place. Now, home was a spacious three bedroom, two bath penthouse on the 22nd floor at one of the most prestigious addresses in Manhattan: 100 East 86th Street. Eve, Star Jones, Ruby Dee and Ossie Davis were my neighbors. Things had changed.

I had fallen asleep on the living room sofa. The last thing I remembered, I was watching Conan O'Brien. Madison, the six month old Pit Bull that I had brought as a gift for myself was spread out on the off white carpet right next to me.

"Good morning, Madison," I said in a hoarse and dry voice. "Good morning," I repeated. Madison popped her head up and playfully rubbed it on my legs. "How's Mommy's girl today? Huh?"

After I played with Madison, I got up and walked toward the floor to ceiling windows which revealed a breathtaking view of Central Park. I would often find myself looking out of that window for hours. The view always calmed my spirit whenever I got caught up in the drama that the streets would often pull me into.

Living so high up made me feel invincible—like I was protected and shielded from the rest of the world.

I don't feel like going anywhere today. I thought as I walked toward my bedroom. When I entered my room, my eyes had instantly landed on my off-white chaise. The sight immediately annoyed me -- it was overflowing with clothes that needed to be dry cleaned. I made a mental note to call Rosa, my housekeeper. She had asked for three days off. One day had passed and already things were totally out of order. I hated it, but not enough to trust anyone else to clean my home. Rosa would just have to cut short her time off.

My bedroom was my sanctity. It was lavishly decorated in warm earth tones. Candles in every size and scent were scattered around the room. The bed was a custom made king size four-poster bed imported from Italy. My favorite pastime was lying next to the gas fireplace listening to music.

* * *

CHA-CHING

It was 11:38. The morning was just about gone and I needed to meet with Pam and Black. I hit the speaker button and began dialing Pam.

The call went straight into voicemail. "Unh Unh Unh...*my* minutes. Yo, if you see yourself calling me over and over...and I'm not picking up, that's because you're not worth my minutes. Take it personal!"

"Pam, it's me...Storm. I called your ass twice last night and you never called me back. You don't want *me* to take it personal, I know. Call me back."

Then I decided to call Black. He was one of my main connects. He supplied me with names, social security numbers, date of births, addresses – the whole nine yards. I never understood why or for that matter how Black got into the game. Black had a Masters in computer technology. He was smart and could passionately engage in topics ranging from politics, to science, and sports. The rumor was he had extorted money from a top Fortune 500 firm and did a heavy bid for it. When he was released from jail, he amped up his game and took his computer knowledge and prison education to the streets.

"Hey, Storm."

"Hey, Black. What's going on?"

"Ain't shit. What's good with you?"

"Just trying to hook up and see what's up."

"A'ight. What time you trying to do that?"

"Is one good for you?"

"Yeah. That's cool...that's cool. Where at?"

"Junior's?"

"A'ight. I'll holla at you then."

"One."

As soon as I put the telephone back on the receiver it rang. I looked at the Caller ID – it was Pam. I picked it up on the first ring.

"Where the fuck you been at?" I asked.

"Girl, you don't *even* wanna know," Pam said.

"What happened?"

"You know that tall black nigga I met last week at Taj's spot?"

"Yeah…Rocky?"

"Rock," Pam corrected.

"I don't know why you even bother with someone with that kinda name anyway. You were with him?"

"Yeah, girl," Pam sighed heavily. "I went over to his house last night and the nigga had me walk into his house backwards. Talking about he have to make sure I don't bring no bad spirits in his house and shit. I should have left then. But it was two o'clock in the morning and I ain't feel like driving all the way back home…'cause he live way out in Rosedale somewhere right next to Green Acres Mall."

"Pam! Go on and just tell me what happened…damn. I hate when you do that."

"Okay! Anyway, I ain't even gonna get into the freaky shit he was trying to have me do. I'll tell you about that later. But let me tell you…gurrrrl…since I left this nigga house I've been sick and I ain't have nothing but bad luck. He musta reverse the shit on *me!*"

"Don't tell me you ate his food."

"Nah. But don't you know...I'm driving on Southern State ready to get off on the Conduit and this car from outta nowhere came and wrecked my shit up."

"Get the fuck outta here! Stop playing!"

"I ain't playing. And that ain't all either. The cops gave *me* a fucking ticket 'cause they said I didn't yield. I ain't never got no ticket before. And the bad part about it is homeboy car didn't have a scratch on it. But he wrecked up my shit. Now how that happen?"

"What? The car is messed up bad?"

"The shit is *totaled* Storm!"

"Did you get hurt?"

"No, I'm okay. I'll probably be hurting tomorrow though. I'm just shaken up. That's all. I can't believe this shit. I ain't have the car a good month."

"Don't sweat it though. That nigga ain't do nothing to you," I said with a small chuckle, "it's just a coincidence."

"Storm, if I tell you the rest of the story...you ain't gonna say that. Believe me."

"Well, tell me later I need to start getting dress."

"All right. What time you trying to hook up?"

"One o'clock at Junior's."

"Okay."

"So wait a minute...did they tow your car?"

"Yeah. I'ma go get me a rental later on."

"Where you at now?"

"I'm downtown...trying to find me something to wear. I'm going to see Mary perform tonight."

"Oh, I forgot you were going to the Mary J. concert tonight. Pam, Is it cold out?"

"Hell, yeah. It's freezing out this bitch."

"Okay, so you want me to have Rick pick you up?"

"Nah, that's okay...I'll probably be still downtown shopping and I can just walk on over to Junior's. Anyway, how was Rick gonna pick me up? Taj is outta town?"

"Yeah. He's in M.I.A. He'll probably be back later on tonight."

"Alright, girl. Well, let me go. I'll see you at one o'clock then."

"Okay, bye."

I stood in the center of my closet, scanning around hoping that eventually something would scream at me to wear. After pondering for several minutes, I finally decided on a black Dolce & Gabana shirt and slacks with my grey and black Prada sneakers. Then I went into the fur closet adjacent to the master closet and took my black waist length Chinchilla off of the hanger.

I stared at the mirror. I had to admit...I was one bad bitch. I was often mistaken for Stacey Dash—but the truth was I looked better than her. Admiring my physique, I turned to the side to get a better view of the six pack on my stomach. Although I was a perfect size five. I wasn't always satisfied with the flatness of my stomach. Four months ago, I hired a personal trainer, and the results were becoming more noticeable. The pain was finally paying off.

* * *

CHA-CHING

I climbed inside of my 2003 black on black X5, selected the CD function and suddenly Alicia Keys was singing *Fallin'*. Immediately I began to think of Taj. He had been gone only two days but I was missing him badly.

Taj and I met two years ago at Capital City, the club he owned, located downtown Brooklyn. Although past experiences had led me to resign myself to flying solo, it was a challenge that I couldn't win staying away from him.

Taj was six feet two inches with a chiseled and buffed body. He had smooth dark skin, his long and thick eyelashes accentuated his brown eyes. Taj's lips were like Denzel's and he had pretty white teeth. It didn't take long to learn that he also possessed all the qualities I demanded my man to have—style, street smarts, power and plenty of money.

I reached for my cell phone to call Taj. As soon as I picked up the phone, it began to ring – it was Taj.

"Hey, baby," I said. "I was *just* getting ready to call you."

"What's really good, ma?"

"Nothing...missing you."

"Yeah. I miss you, too. Where you at?"

"In the car. I'm heading to Brooklyn. I gotta meet Black and Pam."

"That's what's up."

"When you coming back, Taj?"

"I'm leaving tonight."

"Good. What flight are you gonna catch?"

"I think it's leaving Miami at 6:15. But if I don't make that one, I think there is another one leaving at 8:30."

"Why you don't think you can make the 6:15 flight? I need for you to come back home."

"Storm, I gotta make sure dude get on the train and everything go okay...what you mean you *need* me back home."

I laughed. "I meant what I said. I'm missing you big time, baby. You know I don't like being alone too long."

"Oh, so Madison ain't keeping you company."

"Taj!"

"Well, I ain't know...I mean you be giving that dog more attention than me sometimes."

"Whatever, Taj."

"Has Rick been keeping in touch with you?"

"Yeah. I heard from him yesterday."

"A'ight. Make sure you call him if you need him."

"Okay, I will. Oh, did you let him know what time you're coming in tonight?"

"Nah, I'll call him though. Don't worry about that. I got that."

"All right. Let me go. I'll call you later on."

"Love you."

"Love you, too."

* * *

When I arrived at Junior's, Black, Pam and this chick named Shade was already there.

"Hey, what's up y'all?" I asked.

"Hey, what's up, Storm?" Shade responded.

"What's going on girl?" Pam asked.

CHA-CHING

"You don't know how to speak nigga?" I asked Black.

"My bad," Black apologized. Then he directed his attention back to his telephone call. "Yo, listen I'll hit you back later." Black walked over and embraced me. "What's up baby girl? You looking fine as usual."

"Thanks, boo," I said. Why y'all ain't get a table?"

"We just got here," Pam proclaimed.

I nodded at Shade then turned to Pam "What she doing here?"

"Oh, I ran into her at Macy's."

"Get rid of her!"

Pam gave a nervous laugh. "You ain't right Storm."

"I ain't playing. Get rid of her. You know you don't do no shit like that."

"She's taking me uptown after we leave here."

"Pam what part don't you understand? I don't care if she's taking you to Timbuktu...she ain't sitting down eating at no table with me."

Pam caught an instant attitude. I knew that eventually she would. It never failed. Pam always seemed to have a hard time accepting orders from me. I always reminded her that business was business and friendship was a separate entity. I didn't get where I was mixing the two.

"Well, she gonna have to sit in her car 'cause I'm not trying to take no train uptown. It's too cold to be riding the train. Are you going back home once you leave here?"

"Unh Uh...I gotta few stops to make. Just make the bitch wait in the car. I mean what's the problem? You're wasting my time standing here debating over small shit."

Pam walked away, whispered something to Shade, then Shade left.

* * *

"Pam, we got the work when you gonna get busy?" I asked.

"Tomorrow," Pam said. "We doing VA."

I tore off a piece paper out of my Louis Viutton planner and jotted down a few items. "Here is the list of what I want."

"Okay."

"You got your pictures?"

"Yeah. I met up with Juan. He got some phat DLs from VA. Them shits look original."

"I met this dude the other day that do some good work, too." Black interjected. "I can give you his number."

"Ain't this your personal list?" Pam asked. "Where's the client list?"

I dug in my handbag and retrieved the other list of items. "Here. We need some nice electronics...three plasmas. Jewelry...some nice pieces...especially bracelets. Listen when you go OT, make sure you stop at Tysons Corner at Zella's. Ask for Muhammad. That's my peoples. He's gonna let you do the damn thing."

"A'ight."

"You gonna get 40 off of this. And get yourself a couple of cards when you go to Macy's."

"I'ma take Shade with me. And I'ma hit her off with a little something."

"I don't give a fuck if you buy her a car, just bring me my shit."

"Pam, why you fucking with that bitch?" Black asked. "She just trying to get on. Her baby father is on and he ain't even fuckin' with her."

"Nah, that bitch gonna earn her keep. Ain't no loafing. She gotta get up. She know what time it is. Fuck that. Storm, anything else?"

"We good."

Black clasped his hands. "Y'all ready to order? Let's eat."

Looking at the menu, I said, "Me, too. I'm feeling for some grits and sunny side eggs today."

"You the only person I know that will eat grits anytime of the day," Pam said.

* * *

After we ate, Pam got into the car with Shade. Black and I walked to the Park Right parking lot around the corner from Albee Square Mall.

"Yo, Storm, I know Pam's your girl and all, but you better watch out, 'cause she got larceny in her heart."

"I can trust her, Black. She's got my back."

"I'm telling you Storm...keep your eye on her. I don't trust her. That bitch will cut your throat."

"I appreciate you looking out but Pam is cool," I defensively replied. "I've known her for a minute. She's one of the few people I can trust. She's good people. Anyway, so when you gonna have some more work for me."

"I'm gonna hit up one of the credit report agencies by the end of the week. I'll hit you off by Friday."

"That'll work." I reached in my pocket and pulled out a stack of crisp one hundred dollar bills. "Here."

"Thanks."

Chapter 6

I turned over and snuggled closer to Taj, then kissed him on the back of his neck. "Why are you up so early?"

"I couldn't sleep...my stomach hurts," Taj answered.

I put my hands on his stomach and began to rub it. "What's the matter?"

"I think it was that Mexican food we had last night. I can't be messing with you, Storm. You always trying to eat different shit."

"I'm sorrreee. I thought you like trying different things."

"Yeah," Taj grimaced, "but my stomach ain't trying to have it."

I climbed out of the bed. "I'll go make you a cup of tea."

"I don't want no tea."

"Why you trying to give me a hard time this morning?"

"Storm, come on now."

"Come on now what?"

"Okay...okay. I'll take a cup of tea. Damn, girl."

"And a slice of toast...and some Pepcid."

Taj laughed and yelled out as I walked out the room. "I don't need another mother."

"And I ain't trying to be one. By the way, your mother said to call her."

"When she call here?"

"Early this morning. She said it wasn't important...just checking on you."

"A'ight, I'll call her later."

The phone began to ring.

"I can't find the other cordless phone in here," I yelled from the kitchen. "Answer the phone."

"It's Pam."

"Okay. I'm coming," I said walking toward the bedroom.

"Here," Taj said handing me the telephone.

"Hey, what's up?"

"Girl, you know I had mad drama yesterday," Pam said.

"What happened?" I asked.

"I was in Circuit City and opened up a joint."

"Hold up...where you at?"

"I'm on the Turnpike."

"You ain't back home yet?"

"Nah, Shade wanted to stop by her family house in Maryland first. We ended up staying the night there."

"So you had drama yesterday in Circuit City but you just telling me *today*?"

"Storm, I tried calling you about five times yesterday."

"Pam, I checked my voicemails...and I ain't have not one message from you."

"I didn't leave a voicemail."

"Then you didn't call."

"I did call."

"I said if you ain't leave no message, you ain't call. And if you couldn't reach me on one of the cell phones why didn't you try and two-way me? I mean what's the point of me buying you all that shit to keep in touch with me if you ain't gonna use none of it?"

"I tried to direct connect you...and you ain't answer that either. It kept saying, 'the Nextel customer you are trying to reach—"

"Whatever, Pam. I'm not even gonna keep going back and forth with you on this. You didn't call and you know you didn't!"

"Storm, how you gonna—"

I quickly interrupted her. "I said I'm finished. Now tell me what the fuck happened at Circuit City!"

"Baby, calm down," Taj whispered.

"Like I was saying, I went into Circuit City and opened up a joint. They gave me 10Gs. I bought a 35-inch plasma, and a couple of lap tops. I get to the register...and the bitch was ringing me up and all of sudden, she stopped to make a call. She wearing a funny look on her face and I know her ass is up to something. Then she said she had to verify some information. So, I'm waiting and waiting while she is doing her thing. She was on the phone so long that I knew something wasn't right. Next thing you know...I see a fake toy cop walking up front. So I just bounced. You know that ain't worth getting knocked for."

"So wait a minute...you ain't get *shit*?"

"I did...I mean not at Circuit City. But I went to Best and got 10Gs from there."

"You must've been sloppy, Pam. You let triflin' ass Shade through your game off."

"Storm, come on now, why you trippin'? Ain't shit happen. I got the shit."

"*I'm* trippin'? You know what? I ain't even doing this right now. Anyway, what else happened?"

"Oh," Pam's voice grew with excitement. "I got 20Gs from Zelle's. Muhammad hooked me up! I racked up on some canary diamonds, tennis bracelets...and girl guess what I got for myself?"

"What?"

"Some Iced out boogas for my ears."

"Oh, yeah."

"Well, damn, what's up with that Storm? Didn't you say I could get something?"

I chose to ignore her. "Did you go to Macy's and get the gift cards?"

"Yeah, I stopped at Crystal City. I got a stack of ones and few for five."

"I told you to get all of them for five. I ain't trying to waste no time with fifty dollar profits. Shit I spend that much on my stockings." I sighed heavily. "I guess I'll see you when you get back."

"Okay, I should be back around 12. I'ma drop Shade off, then I'll come by your place."

"Nah. Call me first. I don't know where me and Taj gonna be today. I might have to just meet you somewhere."

"A'ight. Is it still snowing there?"

"I didn't know that it snowed. It wasn't snowing when I came in last night."

"Yeah, it's snowing here. I think New York supposed to get eight inches or something like that."

"Oh, that's why Madison so quiet this morning. She probably just sitting, and staring out the window."

"You ain't take her out for a walk yet?"

"Nah, I'm getting ready to do that now."

"Well, be careful out there."

"You, too."

"I'll call you when I get back in town."

"Hmmm, hmmm." I slammed down the telephone. Then I turned to Taj. "She is starting to piss me off."

"Just calm down. You know what you do when you see her, just let her know that you don't like the way she rolling lately. This is your show. You're the maestro of this shit. Just put the bitch in her place. I told you a long time ago to get rid of her ass. She be trying to take advantage 'cause she know y'all cool. You need to put that friendship shit aside. You can't do business and be friends with a bitch. Your shit is too tight...she probably hating a little bit, you never know."

"Black told me the same thing the other day."

"What...about Pam?"

"Yeah. He told me to be careful."

"I'm not saying all of that. She ain't gonna cross you or nothing like that. She ain't that crazy. But she probably dragging her feet a little bit 'cause she think she got it like that. She probably getting a little comfortable you know? She see you looking fine as shit sitting on your millions and she think you can cross her legs, too."

"Well, whatever it is, I'm nipping it today."

"That's all you gotta do. Refresh her memory with the rules."

The telephone rang.

"Hello," I said.

The caller hung up. I looked at the Caller ID. It read "Unknown."

"Who was that?"

"I don't know. Those hang up calls are starting up again."

"Yo', why you looking at me like that? I ain't got nobody calling here hanging up on you."

"A guilty conscious needs no accusing."

"What?"

"You heard what I said. This shit betta not be starting up again."

"Storm, why every fucking time somebody call and hang up, it's my fault?"

"Because that is the shit *your* bitches do."

"Bitches? One bitch...Denise. One mistake that you won't let a nigga live down."

"'Cause the shit won't go away."

"Storm, I ain't talk to that girl in over a year. I wish you would stop bringing her ass up. You letting a bitch fuck up your head!"

"You bought her up...I didn't."

"You ain't say her name but *you* brought her up. Listen, I ain't gonna argue with you over something that happened a year ago. I'm getting in the shower."

"You ain't gonna drink your tea?"

"You drink it!"

I jumped off the bed and wrapped my arms around him. "I'm sorry."

"Let go of me."

"Taj, I said I'm sorry."

"I'm tired of that shit. I know you had a rough childhood and shit and I try and be patient with you because of that...but you be trippin'. Your ass is pissed with Pam and you starting shit with me over a hang up call. I ain't have nothing to do with that. I told you a hundred times to get call intercept or whatever the hell that thing is. Then you won't have nobody calling here with a block number. You letting the bitch win 'cause you sitting there spazin' over it and shit."

"Taj, baby, I'm wrong."

"Storm, you gotta stop with the accusations. I ain't out there messing with nobody. That's the past. I know I hurt you and I ain't trying to put you through that shit again. What we got I can't get from anywhere. You gotta trust me."

"I do trust you."

"You don't."

"Can we just forget about it?"

"You can't keep bringing that shit up," Taj continued.

"I won't. I promise. Now let's stop talking about it. I'ma go and take Madison for a walk."

"I'll do it. I looked out the window, its looks real bad out there."

"Thanks. I'll go and make us breakfast then."

"On second thought, you go ahead and walk Madison and I'll make the breakfast."

We both laughed. "You ain't right," I said.

Taj two-way began to vibrate.

"What's wrong?"

"Nothing," Taj said while typing. "Rick wanted to know if I needed him."

"Where you going?"

"I'm not going anywhere, Storm. I just two-wayed the man back and told him he didn't have to worry about driving me anywhere today 'cause I'm chilling with my wife. You see what I mean?"

"Go on and walk Madison." *Damn, I am trippin'.*

While Taj was gone, I laid across the bed. I must have fallen asleep. Taj woke me up nibbling on my ear.

I'm smiled and pulled him on top of me. "You back?"

"Yup," Taj got up and pulled me up off of the bed. Come on let's go outside."

"Why?"

"Let's go to Central Park. I see all the kids out there playing."

"I ain't trying to watch no kids play, Taj."

"Why you be acting like that Storm? Come on."

"You know I don't like snow and I ain't crazy 'bout no kids."

"And I can't understand that shit either."

"I told you before my mother named me Storm because of a hurricane. She probably ain't know what the hell she was doing. Trust me it didn't have nothing to do with a snowstorm."

Taj pulled me out of the bed. "Get dressed."

"I'm tired."

"I said, get dressed. Come on now."

* * *

Taj and I had a good time. We played catch football and made angels in the snow. All the simple things I missed out doing as a child. Sometimes I had a hard time absorbing what a perfect man Taj was. Yes, he had his faults like the next man but Taj Anderson knew how to love Storm Williams. That in itself took perfection.

"Baby, you want some ice cream?" I called from the bedroom.

"Uhhh...did you pick up some Orange Sherbet?" Taj asked.

"Yeah."

"A'ight. You can give me a little."

"Okay."

"Ma, where's that lotion that I like? I don't see it."

"It's in there, Taj. Look in the closet there. It should be on the second shelf with all the other lotions and soap."

"I see it."

When I came back into the bedroom Taj was underneath the covers flipping channels.

"Here," I said handing him the bowl.

"Thanks. What you got?"

"My usual."

"I don't know how you eat that...raw cookie dough mixed in with ice cream."

"It's good," I declared positioning myself on his lap. "When I was a kid I used to steal the Pillsbury cookie dough and eat it just like that. Sometimes it was breakfast, lunch and dinner. Miss LT used to call me Cookie because I loved it so much," I chuckled.

"That's why I can't understand why you like it now. You should be tired of it."

"I did get tired of it for a while. I stopped eating it for a few years but now since they mixed it with the ice cream—"

"That's like one summer I spent down south with my Aunt Carolyn, she used to love Fig Newton cookies. Man...that was the only kind of sweets she would bring into that house. I would eat so much of those cookies 'til I end up getting sick one day and threw up all over the place. Since then I ain't never ate another Fig Newton."

We both laughed. "I love listening to you talk about your childhood."

"Why?"

"Because you can talk about it and laugh. Even when you talk about getting sick 'cause you ate too many of those cookies...it wasn't 'cause you didn't have no other choice but to eat that. You know what I mean? *You* have memories that make you smile."

"Storm, I wish I could take away what happened to you. All I can say is we're together now...and *together* we gonna make memories that will make the both of us smile."

I reached over and kissed him. "Damn, I just love you, boo."

Ring Ring

"Don't answer that."

I glanced at the Caller ID. "It's Pam. I need to take it."

"Put that phone down! It can wait 'til tomorrow."

"Taj."

"Nah, we chilling tonight. I wanna talk."

I scooted to rest my back on the headboard. "What's wrong? Why you got so serious all of the sudden?"

Taj got out of the bed and started to roll up. "Storm, we gotta talk about how you be flippin'."

"What are you talking about?"

"You not trusting me...being paranoid all the time and shit."

"I'm not paranoid. You talking about what happened this morning?"

"I'm talking about this morning and what happens almost every time I go to the club...which you seem to forget is *my* club. That's my bread and butter. I ain't going there to chill with my boys—I'm there building. I'm there working toward our future. Yet, you always accusing me and shit. I try to understand and be patient with you. I know you had a hard time and shit. But damn, baby, you gotta let it go."

"What…so what you trying to leave me?"

"Leave you? Storm, I'm trying to love you. All of you. But you won't let a nigga love you."

"What are you saying? How am I stopping you from loving me?"

"You got this shield around you…you let me in a little bit. But you always guarding yourself like you gotta be careful with me. You say you love me, but you ain't trusting me enough to love you."

"What do you want me to do? I mean, what do you want from me, Taj?"

"I want you to open up," Taj calmly replied. "I want you to let me in…totally. If that means letting me in…let me in. Not a little bit, not when you think I won't judge you. All the time. I don't know what you're scared of but I'm not gonna judge you, Storm. I want to love all of you, not just the part you feel comfortable sharing and showing me."

"What do you want to know?" I yelled. "You wanna know how fucked up my life was? Huh? That's what you wanna to know? You already know that. You wanna know all about how I fucked to feed myself? Or, no…I know…you wanna know how I fucked and sucked dirty ol' men dicks to support my Aunt Hope and her dopefiend ass man habit. Right? And you wanna talk about love? Huh? Let's talk about how much love I got. Well…love for me was a holiday that was *never* celebrated. That was love. That was *my* life! But you know what? The bad that was interjected in me was for goodwill. Don't you agree?" I asked ferociously. "Look at how successful I turned out to be. I'ma black hoe that got rich in the credit card game. I'm the symbol of success...straight out of mothafuckin' Bushwick."

Taj sat with his mouth open. He may have suspected it, but until that moment he never knew how deeply layered the pain was, nor the ugly past that I harbored. "I'm...I'm sorry," Taj said choking back tears.

"What are you sorry for?" I wiped away the single tear that managed to escape from my eye. "You ain't do nothing."

"You know what? Forget it. I don't want you to hurt like this."

"No, no. It's okay. I'm fine. Maybe you're right. Maybe I need to talk about it and then maybe it'll stop hurting. I need to talk about the fact that other than Miss LT, ain't nobody ever give a fuck about me."

There was suddenly an awkward silence. "What about your mother?"

I chuckled in disgust. Then I took the blunt from Taj and took a couple of drags. "You know, I never told you...my mother was a mortician."

"A mortician? Word? Stop playin'.'"

"Yeah, I'm serious." I smiled. "I was told that she always suffered from depression—but she was religious. I remember her taking me to church and singing hymns around the house. Aunt Hope always told me that we're not suppose to handle the dead-- when they go that's it. We suppose to wrap their bodies and bury them. Being a mortician, you handle all these bodies and some of the spirits are bad—demonic. They say that one day Momma embalmed a man's body that had raped and killed about two or three little girls.

"Aunt Hope always said when Momma opened up his body--the demons jumped out of his soul and got a hold of Momma. After that, Momma cracked up and started messing with my father who was a drug pusher. I never knew his real name. In fact, I didn't know anything about him other than he supplied the dope that pushed Momma permanently into darkness.

"My mother was so smart, and beautiful, you know?" I said my voice cracking. "She had smooth cooper-tone skin. I remember she was tall and had hazel eyes--like me." I managed to smile at the gradually fading memory of her. "But her eyes were prettier...more on the green side. She had a real thick scar on her hand that kinda looked like a lobster. I think my father pushed her into a glass door or something. And I remember she always wore a certain kind of perfume. I'm not sure of the name, but I won't ever forget the smell. It was a soft and light scent. I've only smelt it on one person before--an old lady on the bus was wearing it. Anyway, you know the rest...one Christmas she left to go to the grocery store and never came back."

Taj pulled me toward him and tightly embraced me. "I'm so sorry, boo, because you didn't deserve that childhood hell. And you sure don't deserve the life sentence of pain."

Chapter 7

Opening up to Taj proved more therapeutic than I could have ever imagined. For years, I had convinced myself that I had divorced that part of my life. I never knew how much my past affected me and most of all, how much it dictated my future.

I reached over to Taj and he wasn't there. Then I began rubbing the sleep out of my eyes. I squinted to gain eye focus to read the time on the cable box: 9:34 a.m. *Damn. It's that late?*

"Taj," I called out. "Taaaaaaaj, baby what you doing?"

Madison came running into my room barking. "Not you. I ain't call you."

After receiving no answer I began climbing out of the bed. As I started walking toward the bathroom, I noticed an envelope with Taj's handwriting. It was lying at the bottom of bed. *What the fuck is this all about? I shoulda known he wasn't gonna be able to handle all that shit...*

I picked up the envelope:

Hey Beautiful,

Had to take care of something. Call me when you get up. Before you do though, be prepared to answer this...

Will you marry me?

Taj

My hands began to tremble...fate had finally decided to show up. Instead of running to pick up the phone, I headed to the shower. Taj was everything I wanted and more...but did Taj deserve the shattered past I owned?

The phone began to ring, it was Taj.

"Where you at?" I asked.

"Huh?" Taj asked bewilderedly.

"Where you at? Why you ain't wake me up before you left?"

"Good morning to you, too...damn!"

"Good morning," I mumbled.

"You ain't see the note I left you?"

"Yeah...but you ain't say where you was going?"

"Oh, so that's all you gotta say about my note?"

I was silent and started to pick with my fingernails. *I need to get a manicure today.*

"Storm!"

"What? Why you screaming at me like that?"

"What? You know what? Fuck this!"

"Taj! Taj. Oh, I know he ain't just hang up on me." I started to redial his number.

"What?" Taj answered.

"Why you hang up on me? What kind of stupid shit you on this morning?"

"Storm stop calling me." Taj said and then hung up again.

I kept dialing him back, but he kept putting me straight into voicemail. "Fuck you then…you ain't give me a chance to say shit!"

"Miss Storm, are you okay in there?" Miss Rosa yelled from the living room.

"Yeah. When did you get here?" I snapped.

"I just got here. How are you today?"

"I'm fine. How are you?"

"I'm doing won-der-ful," Miss Rosa always sang her words. "It is such a beau-ti-ful day. Would you like me to prepare you some breakfast before I get to work?"

"No, I'm fine." *She is just too damn happy.* "I'll grab something while I'm out. Can you make sure you pick up my clothes from the cleaners? The ticket is on the refrigerator."

"Okay, I will."

Ring, Ring.

"Miss Rosa, can you get that for me? If it's Taj tell him I'm not here."

"Miss Storm, it's the nursing home."

"The nursing home?"

"Yes."

"Okay. I'll pick up the phone in my bedroom."

* * *

"I'm leaving...I'll probably be back before you leave," I announced.

"Is everything alright with your aunt?" Miss Rosa asked.

"I don't know," I answered nervously. "They said she won't eat and she keep asking for me. You know how she is though...she'll do anything for some attention."

"Here, take her this." Miss Rosa handed me a plastic Tupperware container with a huge smile on her face. "It is her favorite...cho-co-late cake. I baked it last night for you."

"Thanks," I smiled back. "I'm sure she'll eat this with no convincing."

* * *

I wasn't prepared to see Miss LT in the state that she had forced herself in. I wasn't ready for why she had been calling for me. I was never taught how to say goodbye. Folks usually left my life without saying it. No one had ever loved me enough to grant me the closure that came with that single word.

Grabbing her hand, I looked up at the nurse, "How long she's been like this?"

"Since yesterday morning."

"What happened? She was fine when I was here two weeks ago."

"I don't know, Ms. Williams. She just took a turn for the worst. The doctor examined her and said he couldn't find nothing wrong. He think she is just giving up."

I quickly wiped the single tear that fell from my eyes. "I pay y'all a lot of money to take care of her. Why didn't somebody call me sooner?"

"I don't know. I can't answer that."

I looked at her name tag. "You don't know shit, do you Miss. Taylor? You don't know what's wrong with her. You don't know why she's sick. What do you know? Huh? I'll tell you what...why don't you go and make yourself useful and find me the motherfuckin' person in this bitch that can answer some damn questions. And on your way, send somebody in here to help me get my aunt dressed. I'm taking her home with me!"

As Nurse Taylor began to walk out of the room, Miss LT began to moan.

"Hey, Miss LT. Why you trying to scare me? If you wanted to see me you know all you had to do was ask? I'ma take you home with me. Okay?"

Miss LT began to clear her throat. "No," she whispered.

"What? What you say?"

"I don't...I don't want to go home with you...this here...this here is my home," Miss LT stammered.

"Well, just come home with me for a few days then. They ain't taking care of you like they suppose to."

"I'm fine, baby. I'm fine right here...'specially since you're here now."

I rubbed her hair and began playing with her long thick braids. "Who did your hair?"

"You did."

"I didn't put these braids in. These are underbraids, you know I don't know how to underbraid, Miss LT."

Miss LT chuckled, "Oh, that's right. That young fast ass girl that works here at night did it. I don't think you met her before."

"Oh, nah, I don't think I have. Anyway, they need to get redone. I'll redo it in a few. Look what I brought you...some of Miss Rosa's chocolate cake."

"I ain't hungry."

"Miss LT you gotta eat. They said you ain't ate nothing in two days. You can't do that. You gotta eat something. Please, just a little piece. Do it for me."

"Storm, sit down."

"Why?" I asked defensively.

"Storm!"

I ignored her and walked away toward the window and pushed the drapes open. Then I turned to Miss LT. "What's wrong?"

"Why you chasing him away?"

"Who?"

"Your young man. Why you chasing him away? He's a *good* man, Storm."

"How do you always know? No matter where I am, you always know? And don't tell me that story about how you were born with a veil over your face."

Miss LT ignored me. "You gotta trust him."

"I do trust him."

"You're lying," Miss LT retorted. "No, you don't. He ain't the one you need to be watching out for."

"What do you mean?"

"He ain't the one," Miss LT struggled to repeat.

I walked closer to Miss LT, picked up her hand and kissed it. "I need you, Miss LT."

"You'll be fine, chile'. You know how to take care yourself. Just get all those snakes out your closet before they bite."

"I won't be fine without you. What are you trying to say to me?"

"I'm so tired."

"Okay, then. Eat a little piece of this cake. Then you can try and get some sleep."

"Storm, please listen to me...I'm tired," Miss LT repeated with great sternness.

"Miss LT...please, please stop saying that."

"I want you to take care of yourself. You here? I want you to let go of the pain that them sorry ass niggas done gave you. You betta than them. You here what I'm telling you? You didn't sink in the sand that they threw you in, you stood on top and walked bravely across it. Ain't too many women out here can say they done been where you came from and blessed enough to be on top.

"Remember, anger don't complete the woman you are...it takes away from the whole strong woman you done become."

I never thought of my survival as being brave, I thought. "I will. I'll let go. Miss LT, I love you."

"I love you, too. You the daughter I always wanted."

"Miss LT?"

"Yes, baby."

"Please don't leave me," I selfishly begged. "Please don't die."

"I'ma always be with you Storm. I'ma always be where you are."

"Miss LT, please stop talking this crazy shit!" I cried.

Miss LT suddenly began to cough. "Storm can you go and get me some water."

I reached for the pitcher and began to pour her a glass.

"No, baby, dat...dat water there ain't fresh. Go on down the hall and get me some fresh water."

"Okay," I pulled the colorful crocheted blanket that Miss LT had created over the white sheet. "I'll be right back."

"Thanks, baby."

I came back into the room, carrying a pitcher full of ice water. "Miss L--noooooooooo."

Chapter 8

Since Miss LT had died, I had trouble sleeping. Although I was grateful that I had the chance to say goodbye, I still felt like I had been cheated. I felt so empty inside. Every night I laid in the bed waiting for her energy to return--anything I just wanted to feel her presence, but I didn't.

"What you gonna do today?" Taj asked.

"I don't know. I'm probably gonna meet Black later on. He got some work for me."

"That's good, ma. You back on the grind. That's what's up."

"I guess. What are you gonna do?"

"Well, you know, I gotta meet dude and pick up this paper. Then I'm gonna go check on a few things at the club. Why? You wanna do something later on?"

"Well, I'm hanging out with Pam and the girls later on tonight. They trying to shake off this funk I've been in and shit. I was thinking about doing some Christmas shopping later."

"Christmas shopping? Not you. You hate Christmas."

"Yeah, I know. But I know it's a big deal for you...so I want to try and get into...for you."

"Uh...A'ight, we can do that," Taj agreed and returned a smile.

"What time you gonna be back?"

"I should be back about two or three."

"Taj that's so late to start shopping."

"No, it's not."

"Yes, it is. You know I need about six to seven hours."

"So what you wanna do? You wanna go tomorrow instead?"

Running my hands through my hair, I answered, "I gotta get my hair done tomorrow."

"Ain't nothing wrong with your hair. Didn't you just get it done? I mean, you can wait one more day and get it done on Monday."

"You know Raphael is not open on Mondays."

"A'ight. I'll try and be back about one. Just make sure you ready."

I walked over and kissed him. "Thank you."

"Um, hum. You can show me how grateful you are tonight. You know a nigga been feeling a little deprived lately."

"I promise I'ma hook you up, boo."

Taj squeezed my butt. "You know you don't need to hang out with Pam and them to shake off your funk...your man can take care of that for you." Then he pointed to his suddenly erect manhood. "See, look how bad Rock's missing you."

"Go on and get dress," I chuckled, "you keep it up and we ain't never gonna get to the mall."

"I don't give a fuck about no mall right now. Storm, I can't walk around with my shit like this. Look what you did to me. Yo, you gonna have to do *something*."

"I didn't do nothing."

"Shit, you ain't gotta tell me. Come on now!"

"Taj, not right now."

Taj grabbed his clothes and went into the guest room to get dressed. I was pushing away the only person left in the world that gave a damn about me. I knew it. Even with Miss LT's last words of warning echoing in my ear, I didn't know how to stop destroying it.

* * *

After Taj left I turned on the radio and headed in my closet to search for an outfit. Jay Z's, *Song Cry* was playing. I immediately thought of Taj. I don't know why but Jay reminded me of Taj. Not his looks...'cause Taj was fioonnne. Maybe it was the gangsta-I'ma solider-but I'm also a rich-no-nonsense-business mothafucka presence that they both seem to have in common.

I picked up the phone to call Taj, but got his voicemail. "Hey, it's me. I really didn't want nothing. I just was calling to see if you were all right. Guess I'll just talk to you later then. Um...I'll see you at one. Love you." I don't know why, but I sometimes had a hard time simply saying sorry.

I decided to wear my Dolce & Gabbana jeans with a matching black sweater, and my black Louis Vuitton sneakers with my matching purse. It was 1:30 and Taj had not come back home and he wasn't answering my two-way messages nor was he returning my voicemails.

The door bell rang. *Oh, there he is. He must have left his key.* Madison had beat me to the door. "Move out the way, Madison. Who is it?"

"It's me, Storm. Black."

"Black?" I asked opening up the door a little disappointed. "What's up? What you doing here?"

"You told me to come by at one o'clock."

"Oh, shit. Damn. My bad. I totally forgot. Taj and I suppose to be doing a little shopping...it's a good thing, he is running late."

"Oh, so you goin' senile on me now."

"Shut-up. Come on in and have a seat. You want something to drink."

"Nah, I'm cool. Can I spark my blunt?"

"Yeah...matter of fact. Let's go in the den."

* * *

Black took a seat on the black leather swivel chair. "Here go the profiles that I want you to check out. My peoples up at BC Health Insurance gave me these. They all A-1."

"Good. How many is it?"

"Ten."

"Ten?"

"Yeah."

"I wanted more than that. I'm trying to do at least 500Gs for the holidays."

"That ain't no problem. I can call my connect at the bank and have some more profiles for you tomorrow. What you tryin' to do—like 10 more?"

"Yeah, that should be good," I said anxiously looking at my watch.

"Well, damn, ma, that's the third time you looked at your watch in five minutes. What I'm holding you up or something?"

"Nah. I told you Taj and I was supposed to be going out and he ain't back yet. It's not like him to be late."

"Call him then."

"I did. It's going straight into voicemail. You know what...let me try two-waying him again." I began typing: *what's up? I'm waiting on you.*

Fifteen minutes had passed and Taj still had not responded to my message. "He's probably in a bad spot and ain't getting no reception," Black tried to reassure.

"For his sake, he better be," I said with an attitude.

My two-way started to ring. The message was from Taj. It read: *Don't wait. Ain't shit up...u should know that!*

"This nigga is on some real smelly shit right now, huh?"

"What's up?" Black asked.

"Nothing! Not a mothafuckin' thing," Then I threw my two-way across the room. "Let me get a pull."

* * *

By the time Black left it was five o'clock. Pam had been blowing up my cell phone. I wasn't sure if she was looking for work or calling to make plans to hang out. It didn't matter though I wasn't in the mood to be around her. My mind was steady and heavy on Taj. My emotions were flip flopping out of control. One minute, I was sitting there trying to figure out how to make things better between Taj and me, and the next minute, I was talking myself out of gathering his clothes and throwing it out of the window.

I sat on the sofa flicking through the channels. I had called Taj about fifty times and he wouldn't answer any of my calls. Finally, I decided to call Rick and see if he would give me the 411 on Taj.

"Hey, Rick."

"What's up baby girl?"

"Nothing, just chilling. Where y'all at?"

"I'm at my moms right now."

"That's nice, you checking out Mom dukes. Where's Taj?"

"Oh, I dropped him at the club earlier. He said he was gonna have one of the cats there dropped him home. Why...you need something?"

"No. I'm good."

"You sure? You sound like something is wrong."

"No, I'm straight. I'ma get ready and do a little shopping."

"You need me?"

"Yeah, matter of fact I do. You feel like it."

"Now, Storm you know all you gotta do is say the word. What's up with the X5?"

"Nothing. I just don't feel like driving, that's all."

"A'ight. I'll be there in about a half hour."

"Thanks, Rick. You can park in one of the guest spots in my garage and we'll take my truck. Just call me when you get downstairs."

"Okay, baby girl. See you in a bit."

"Bye."

* * *

When I'm feeling down, I like to shop. When I don't give a fuck, I shop using other peoples information.

Rick called, "Hey."

"You downstairs?"

"Yeah."

"I'll be right down."

"A'ight."

I grabbed my waist length Mink and my Louis Vuitton purse and headed out the door.

* * *

"Where we going?" Rick asked.

"To the Village."

"You shopping in the Village this time of the day?"

"No, I gotta get me some IDs."

"Storm! What you doing?"

"Being grown!"

"Okay...okay. I ain't tryin' to have Taj spazzin' on me 'cause I got you out here doing this shit."

"Taj ain't gonna know shit--unless you tell him. Besides, Storm is grown." Whenever I spoke of myself in third person, anyone close to me knew it wasn't worth their time debating with me. "Storm is doing what she *wants* to do. Taj is obviously doing him. So Storm is about to do her."

"Shit, what the fuck have I gotten myself in the middle of," Rick tried to whisper.

* * *

I climbed in my X5 and waited as Rick put the Blarney's bags carefully in the trunk.

"Okay, where we heading to now, Storm."

I crossed my legs and replied, "You mean, Ms. Stocker."

"Huh?"

"Ms. Stocker."

Rick released a soft chuckle. "Girl, you're crazy."

* * *

It was 8:30 and Taj still had not returned any of my calls. My emotions continued to range back and forth from anger to fear. Finally, anger took control and defined my next move.

"Yo, what's up?" I asked.

"Hey, girl. I was just getting ready to call you. Why you been ignoring my calls?" Pam asked. "We still hanging out tonight?"

"Yeah," I answered back. "That's why I'm calling you. Where you tryin' to hang out at?"

"I don't really care. It's on you."

After a few moments, I suggested, "What about Capital City?"

"Cap City? You never want to hang out at Taj's. What's up with that?"

"Ain't nothing up."

"Whatever."

"I'm serious."

"Girl, don't you know I know you betta than that? Guess you'll tell me later then. Anyway, so what time are you gonna be ready?"

"About twelve."

"A'ight."

"I'll come and pick you up. Where you gonna be at?"

"I'ma be at my house."

"Okay, later."

"One."

* * *

Harlym, the bouncer escorted Pam and me to the VIP section. 50 cent and his entourage were also in the house. There was a bucket of ice with a bottle of Cristal on each table. Smoke hovered thick over the barricaded VIP area. An array of Vibe,

XXL, Black Enterprise, and F.E.D.S. magazines covered the round cocktail tables. DJ Clue was holding it down for the night.

It wasn't long before Taj was notified by his staff that I was in the house.

"Hey, what's up, Pam?" Taj said.

"Hey, Taj...what's up?" Pam said.

Then Taj walked closer to where I sat and looked at me. "Storm."

I ignored him and took another pull of the blunt. "Storm, you hear me talking to you," Taj repeated.

"What?"

Taj walked over to me until he stood directly in front, then he grabbed my arm. "Come here."

"Get off of me!" I said as I struggled to free myself from his hold.

"I said come here!"

"Who the fuck do you think you are grabbing me in public like that? I ain't you damn child, Taj. I done told you that shit before."

"Storm, just go see what he want...don't try and make no scene," Pam pleaded.

I looked at Pam then turned my attention back to Taj. "You didn't have shit to say to me for the past eight hours, now 'cause I walk up in *your* club you think you can disrespect me in front of niggas."

"You know what...fuck it!" Taj said releasing the hold he had on my right arm. "You so fucking ghetto." Taj angrily walked away.

"What was that all about?" Pam inquired.

"I don't know."

"What do you mean?"

"I don't know what his fucking problem is. I mean, the nigga got mad 'cause I ain't give him no pussy this morning and he wouldn't take my calls all day. Then when I step up in here, he wanna act like he the man and shit and be salivating all over me...I ain't having that. He lucky 50 was up in here or I would really cut the fool. 'Cause you know Storm don't give a gotdamn!"

Pam was still stuck on the part of me not giving Taj none. "You mean you ain't giving your man none and you don't know what's wrong with him? Then you roll up in his club half naked and you don't know why he's heated. Storm you be asking for an ass whipping...for real!"

"What? This is my shit...if I ain't in the mood, I ain't in the mood. Hell, it's plenty of times I feel like doing shit and he's too tired. You don't see me walking around with my ass on *my* shoulders."

"But Storm you said you ain't been in the mood since Miss LT passed away. Girl, that's been a minute. You can't keep holding out like that."

"Who said I can't? I'm grown. I can do what the hell I wanna do. I tell you what though, if he *was* gonna get some...he blew it now, acting like a damn child."

"Huh?" Pam gave me a look I couldn't define...it was a look I had saw once before, but I couldn't put my finger on what it was all about. "Well, you got a man, Storm. I mean he takes care of you...you don't have to worry about him cheating and shit--"

I quickly interrupted Pam. "What? Bitch, I takes care of me...ain't no man doing that! I've been taking care of myself since I was 12 mothafucking years old--"

"I'm just saying though..."

"What you saying? You know what, Pam? For real, for real...I didn't ask for your opinion, so you can just keep the shit to yourself."

"You know what, Storm?"

"What?" I screamed. "What?"

Pam twisted her lips, then snapped. "Nothing...just forget it."

"Nah, don't stop. Say what you gotta say."

Pam remained silent.

"You can get an attitude if you want to. I came out tonight to have a good time." I threw my hands up in the air in frustration. "I mean damn...you suppose to be lifting a bitch spirits and shit and instead you sitting there clapping and rooting for his ass while he up in here embarrassing me and—"

"How do you feel that I'm rooting for Taj?"

"You are."

"No, I wasn't...Storm you can't stand it when somebody pull your coattail when you're wrong. You ain't always right, you know."

"And I didn't say I was either. Listen, I'm through talking about the shit. Leave it alone." Then I picked up my two-way. "I wonder why Black ain't hit me back yet."

"I thought you was meeting him earlier today."

"I did meet him. He came by the house. But he was suppose to get back to me with some 411 on—Ah...that's my jam right there." I said and stood up, closing my eyes and motioning my body to the beat of Beyoncé and Jay-Z's, *Bonnie and Clyde*. After the record was over, I sat down. "Now I feel bad about arguing with Taj. This joint always make me feel like I wanna fuck all night."

Pam put her hand up. "I ain't even going there with you. What were you about to say Black was getting you the 411 on?"

"Oh...he supposed to be hooking me up with a tiny magnetic card reader. I'm ready to do some other kind of shit, now."

"A tiny magnetic card reader?"

"Yeah. Why the hell are you looking like that?"

"I ain't looking like nothing."

"Oh, yes you are, too. What's up with that? Yo, you on some funny shit tonight."

"Ain't nothing up, Storm. You be bugging. You know that?"

"Oh, trust me when I tell you, I'm not hardly bugging...something's up." Crossing my legs, I added, "Let me find out."

Pam put her glass of Apple Daiquiri down. "Storm, I said ain't nothing up. I'm just surprised you trying to get into that. That's all."

"What's the surprise, Pam? I'm about making money. That right there is gonna make me crazy money. That is gonna take my business to a whole different level. If anything you should be surprised that it took me so long to get on. Matter of fact, I'm surprised you ain't said nothing to me about it yourself. Black told me when he mentioned it to you...you act you was already up on it. Which anyway makes me kinda leary and shit…why wouldn't you say something to me about it?"

"Storm, don't try and sit there and tell me you just getting on now. I know betta than that."

"We ain't talking about when I found out though. We talking about Black saying you knew and you ain't never mentioned it…even just to see where my head was at."

My two-way began to ring. It was Black. *I'm on my way to Cap. C U in a minute.*

"What he say?"

"He's on his way."

"Oh, okay."

* * *

When D'Angelo's, *Lady* came on, Taj walked over to me, grabbed my hand and guided me to the dance floor. That's what I loved about Taj, no matter what, he understands me. He knows what's up and he knew it was up to him to tighten up the game.

When we returned to the VIP area, Black was sitting next to Pam and some other dude I had never met before.

"Hey, what's going on?" I asked.

"Hey. There she go!" Black announced. "What's up, ma?"

"Ain't shit," I answered back.

Then Taj and Black hand greeted each other.

"Storm. This is Shock. Shock this is Storm and her man, Taj. Taj owns this joint."

"Word. That's what's up," Shock said.

"Storm, I gotta check on a few things…I'll be back in a few."

"Okay."

"Storm, I'ma leave in a minute myself. I'm tired."

"Pam, its only 3 o'clock. You ain't even dance tonight."

"I know girl, but girlfriend is tired."

"Wait a minute. Let me get Rick to take you home then."

"Nah, I'm straight. I'ma just hop on the train."

"Pam, calm down, girl. You know I'm not about to let you go home by yourself. I'll get Rick to take you home. Just give me a few minutes."

"Alright."

* * *

Immediately after Pam left, Black started on her.

"Yo, Storm I know you ain't tryin' to hear this but you need to watch out for Pam."

"Why? What's up?"

"I told you she was all up on the magnetic card reader but she was acting like she was slow and shit. You see how fast she got outta here once we got here. She know I peeped her card."

"I told you before that bitch ain't crazy she know better than to try and cross me."

"Storm, I'm telling you she's a snake."

"And I'm telling you, the bitch know she can't dig a grave for me and not get dirt on *her*. Believe me when I tell you, Pam ain't stupid."

Chapter 9

"Boo, you know what I feel like doing today?" I asked joining Taj in the kitchen.

"What?" Taj asked.

"I feel like going ice skating."

Taj flipped the pancake on the other side. "Ice skating?"

"Yeah."

"Yeah? Why you say it like that?"

"I said yeah. That sounds like a plan."

"So you wanna go?"

"Yeah, we can go. Why you in such a good mood today?"

"You ain't for real I know...I mean why I gotta have a reason to be in a good mood? Maybe that Christmas spirit you got going on is beginning to rub off on me."

"Oh, now I *know* something's up?"

"Taj, ain't nothing up. I'm just trying to learn how to enjoy life. That's all. I'm tired of arguing and shit. It got to be more than that to life. I told you last week I'm on some new shit now. You ain't believe me?"

"It's not that I didn't believe you—"

"So why are you acting so surprised?"

"I'm not surprised. I'm proud of you."

"Oh, you are, huh? And you're real smart too…'cause you know just what to say."

"Nah, for real, I'm not playing. I'm saying…I see you making a effort and I wanna thank you. 'Cause I know this time of the year is real hard for you, but you trying to put that behind you and I'm proud of you for that."

"Thank you. Come here and gimme a kiss."

"That's it? You could slip a little tongue in there."

"No, I couldn't have either…'cause you ain't even brush your teeth yet." We both laughed.

"Boo, you need to walk Madison."

"Taj, why you always waiting for me to get up to walk her?"

"Storm, 'cause that's your dog. And don't trip, 'cause you *know* I walk her more than you do."

"But it's nine o'clock in the morning. She should have been out already," I headed to the bedroom to get dress. "No wonder she's acting crazy."

* * *

"Damn, it's cold out here," I said attempting to shake the shivers.

"Look what you got on. You ain't dress warm enough."

"I got on two sweaters. Oh, did anybody call me? I left my cell."

"Yeah. I didn't answer your cell phone but Black and Mimi called on the house phone."

"What Mimi want?"

"She wanna confirm that you still coming in for your massage at one o'clock."

"Today?"

"Yeah."

"I think I got it in my Palm for tomorrow."

"Oh, yeah and Black said call him…it's a 911."

"What's up?"

"He ain't say and I ain't ask him."

"Shit. I don't feel like dealing with no drama today."

"Just call the man and see what's up. Don't get stressed before you even know what he calling about."

I walked to the night table and   picked up the cordless phone from the handset.

"Hey, what's up?"

"Yooooo, one of my peoples called me from VA and said they saw Pam and some other chick on Crimesolvers," Black said.

"WHAT? What for?"

"They said that they got footage of them shopping in some store. I think it was Hay's department store. And bust this? The woman ID they used…she worked for same store."

"You playing?"

"Nah, it's crazy, yo."

"I know that bitch ain't crazy enough to walk in the stores and not be camouflaging and shit. I know she know better than that."

"They say they sure it's Pam. They was showing four different shots of her."

"She is so damn stupid—"

"What happened?" Taj interrupted.

I turned my attention to Taj. "Hay's in VA got Pam's ass on tape charging."

"Oh, shit!" Taj said.

"And bust this? They offering a five thousand dollar reward," Black added.

"Word?"

"You know as much as she goes down there somebody is gonna recognize her and turn her ass in. For five Gs…that's easy money."

I began pacing the living room floor.

"Storm, calm down baby, don't stress it, "Taj urged. Then he stood behind me and gently massaged my shoulders. "Whatever happens…I mean that's on Pam and her dumb ass. You ain't got nothing to do with that."

"Black, listen I'ma talk to you later."

"A'ight. Yo, we need to talk about the other thing."

"What other thing?" Then, I quickly remembered our discussion about the magnetic card reader. "Okay. Well, we can talk about that later. Give me a call later on."

"A'ight."

"Black, listen, just make sure you let me know as soon as you hear anything else."

"You know I will."

"Alright then. Thanks for looking out, Black."

"Hey, now you know I got you, ma."

I hung up and walked over to the sofa, disgusted I buried my face in my hands. "I can't believe she be out here working sloppy. I can't believe this."

"Storm, listen, baby, you don't need to get yourself all stressed about that shit. That's Pam problem. If she went out there and didn't make sure she was correct, it's on her. Why you so nervous?"

"'Cause how I know it ain't gonna come back on me?"

"What do you mean? The only way that shit is gonna come back is if Pam talks if she gets caught. But...you see, see what I be saying."

"What?"

"You don't even trust her ass. That's what. You always defending her ass and I be telling you to watch out for her and now look at you. Look at you! You stressed!"

I couldn't even pretend that I wasn't bothered about Pam possibly talking. "Of course I'm stressed, she works for *me*."

"You need to handle your business. That's all I'm gonna say." Taj started walking to the bedroom.

"I am. Don't worry, Pam's ass is on punishment...believe me when I tell you. Taj? Taj, why you walking away from me? I'm talking to you."

"'Cause I gotta take care of some business. This dude Arrow acting like he want me to bust a nine in his ass."

"But I thought we was gonna go ice skating today."

"We are, later when I get back. Don't you gotta go for your massage?"

"That's right. Make sure you be back by five, Taj."

The telephone rang.

"Storm?"

"Yeah."

"That's your girl on the phone now. You gonna pick up?"

"Yeah, I'll take it. Hello."

"Hey, girl, what's going on?" Pam asked.

"You tell me," I answered dryly.

"Girl, how about me, Peaches and Nina got into a fight at The Tunnel last night."

"A fight?"

"Yeah, girl! We whipped this bitch ass."

"Why?"

"You know how when you in The Tunnel and there be groups of people reppin' their hood?"

"Uh-huh."

"This chick from The Bronx came over to where we were at and started kicking it with Big. You know Nina used to fuck with Big and was kicking it with him. Nina gave her a look like you need to bounce. But the bitch was bold she gonna bump Nina and then have the nerve to bend down to whisper something to Big. Well, you know that was all she wrote. Nina grabbed her no frills weave and started kicking that bitch ass."

"Oh, you made it seem like all y'all had a fight."

"We did. You know we ain't gonna stand there and not jump in."

"Pam, how you sound? If nobody else didn't jump in for the girl why y'all didn't just let the both of them fight?"

"Girl, you know how we do."

"Whatever."

"Damn. What's wrong with you?"

"Oh, nothing really."

"Yeah, right. I can tell something is wrong with you. What? You and Taj had an argument?"

"How can you tell? I mean, you so busy telling me about your fight."

"Storm. What's up with you?"

"That's a question I need to be asking you. You the one shopping and getting caught on tape."

"What? Why you skipping? What the fuck are you talking about?"

"You know what? I ain't going into this over the phone."

"Okay. Well, I'll come over."

"No you not. It's Christmas Eve."

"It's Christmas Eve and you don't celebrate Christmas."

"I am today."

"So, you celebrating Christmas?"

"That's what I said didn't I?"

"So when you gonna meet with me and tell me what the hell is wrong with you?"

"I don't know. Maybe tomorrow," I quickly answered back without thinking that was Christmas.

"Maybe tomorrow?"

"That's what I said right?"

"I thought you had some work for me."

"You thought wrong." I slammed down the receiver. I can tolerate some things, but one thing for certain…I *can't* tolerate anyone or anything jeopardizing my empire.

* * *

After my massage, I called Rick and had him pick me up and take me to 23rd Street to buy a Christmas tree. The salesman decided to give me a mini lesson on Christmas trees. I decided on a six foot Douglas Fur. Finally we stopped at Macy's and I bought twenty boxes of white lights for the tree and two boxes of purple bows to decorate the tree.

The stores were crowded, folks were laughing. Salvation Army's volunteer Santa Clauses' were out in their last attempt to get money for the season. I could see and almost could feel how folks got caught up in the Christmas season.

* * *

By 4:45 p.m. Rosa had the tree decorated. I had turned the radio on to WBLS. They were playing continuous holiday music. Taj's Christmas gifts were neatly under the tree. I had done it.

I heard the key rattling and I hurried in the room to turn off the lights.

"Storm, baby, you here?" Madison ran to Taj.

Then I turned on the Christmas lights. "Merry Christmas!"

CHA-CHING

Taj stood silent. Then I began to cry. I had convinced myself that I was doing all this for Taj. It wasn't until I sang Merry Christmas when I realized that this was for me too....that in my attempt to make Taj happy and finally embrace what we had together, I had set the pain that held me hostage all these years free. Miss LT would be proud.

Chapter 10

"Five."

"Four."

"Three."

"Two."

"One...HAPPY NEW YEAAAAAAAAAA!" The simultaneous clicking of the room full of glasses drowned out the music that was playing. Loads of confetti, and red and white balloons descended from the ceiling.

Taj wrapped his hands around my waist pulled me close, and whispered. "Happy New Year, Storm!"

"Happy New Year, Baby," I said in elation.

"2004 is gonna be *our* year. Bigger and better things are on the way. Anything you want you got."

"I already have everything I want, Taj."

"But it's just the appetizer. The shit we about to eat is the full course meal."

I reached for his hand and kissed it. "You know what? I'm so grateful for you. I always knew I would be successful," I paused and looked around at the crowded room of high rollers and ballers. "Partying here tonight with P. Diddy, and Dame Dash, I mean this ain't no surprise to me. Shit, I *belong* here," I declared with a trace of arrogance. "But I *never* knew I'd have a man in my life that know how to love every corner of me. Somebody I can be free *and* safe with...somebody I can share my world with."

Beyoncé's, *Dangerously in Love* had appropriately begun to play. I quickly turned my back to him, and began passionately grinding him.

Taj put his hands on my waist and rhythmically moved my body with his. Then he began kissing me on my neck until he reached my ear and with his deep sexy voice whispered, "Let's *really* go celebrate...and bring this in the right way."

Even though my Boo is hard as hell on the streets. He knows how to take care of me, I thought. Here I was bringing in the New Year with the man I love, in Miami at the Mercury Resort Spa heading to our penthouse suite. *Life couldn't be better than this.* Without saying a word, I held his hand and followed him as he squeezed and maneuvered off of the dance floor.

Being with Taj always suppressed the memories of my ugly past. It stopped the war that was being fought within me. He had found a way to make this ghetto girl's heart sing. Somewhere in between, the light began to shine.

CHA-CHING

After being together for three years, Taj and I definitely had our share of problems. Neither one of us was ready for love. Hustling does that to you. You get so caught up with winning the game that you don't take the chance of opening up your heart and losing. But we didn't consciously take the gamble on love because love chose us. No matter what we did to get rid of, or ignore it, at the end of the day we were in the thickness of it. The innocence and power of our love—that connection— was totally undeniable.

* * *

When we arrived at our suite, Taj asked me to close my eyes. As he opened the door, I instantly smelled the sweet aroma of flowers. He held my hand and guided me inside, the more steps that I took the stronger the aroma became.

"Alright baby," Taj said, "now you can open your eyes."

I slowly opened my eyes and it was the most beautiful thing I had ever seen. There were roses everywhere. Purple and red rose petals made a trail leading to the balcony. In the living room, there were vases filled with roses. On the cocktail table there was a huge tray of chocolate covered strawberries. My mouth opened but I couldn't speak. I was at a loss for words. I turned my attention to Taj, as we gazed in each other eyes – they were glittering with our love. While the tears rolled down my cheeks, Taj carefully cupped his hands on my face and I placed my hands on top of his. Then he softly kissed my tears.

"Baby, why you cryin'?"

"Because I...I never thought I would be here," I whispered. "I mean I never thought that I could have someone love me like this."

"You know I really love you," Taj said. "You're everything to me, Storm. You're my perfect Storm...just *rain* on me, Baby."

I wrapped my hands around his neck, tip-toped and replied, "And you're the bling bling in my eyes." I walked around the room in amazement, picked up one of the roses and took a sniff. "Baby, when did you have all of this done?"

"Remember when I told you I left my wallet..."

"Yeah. You did this by yourself?"

"Yeah," Taj answered, opened his arms showcasing the floral arrangement. "You ain't know your man could get down like this?"

"I don't know what to say. This is beautiful."

"You ain't gotta say anything. Come on, I got something to show you." Taj grabbed my hand and took the lead following the colorful path of petals that led to the balcony.

"You cold?" Taj asked.

I shook my head. "Nah, I'm okay."

"You *are* cold," Taj turned to walk inside our suite. "I'ma go get you a jacket."

"You don't have to," I said grabbing his hand, "I told you I'm fine. Matter of fact, it feels good out here. But I know one thing...as soon as we get back to New York we gonna be some sick asses. When I spoke to Black earlier he said it was eight degrees there."

"Let's not talk about New York," Taj said while he pulled me toward him as he leaned on the balcony. "I don't want to talk about nothing but us."

We both stared out at the picturesque view. The brightness of the moon's reflection glared on the running waters. I inhaled the smell of the sea. Exhaling I asked, "Isn't this beautiful?"

"Yeah."

"I love the sea, its one of the few places where I feel comfortable at. Did I ever tell you that?"

"You did. I wish I could package it up and hand to you. I love the look on your face when you are here."

"It's the one place in the world that is quiet but not totally. Where you can hear music and no matter what state you were in when you arrived, when you leave peace belongs to you. You know what? I think we should buy a spot down here."

"That's what you want?"

"Yeah, we're down here enough," I said. "I mean it's like a second home now. We could buy a condo or something. What do you think?"

"Anything you want. You know that, ma."

"Taj, why you staring at me like that? You look so serious. What's wrong?"

"Why does something have to be wrong with me admiring my woman's beauty?"

I smiled and tightly embraced him. "Thank you."

"For what?"

"For coming into my life."

Taj turned his attention to the table. "Pour us some of that Cristal."

"Okay." I walked over to the table and reached for the flutes.

"Put some ice in my drink."

"*What*?" I asked. "You know you don't put no ice in *Cristal*."

But Taj insisted, "Just put the ice—*please*." Then he revealed a guilty smile.

As I reached for the ice bucket, I noticed what looked like a piece of ice with metal on it sitting conspicuously on top of the ice cubes. Convinced my eyes were playing tricks on me, I closed them tightly then opened them again. And to my surprise *it* was still there. While my mouth grew instantly dry, and the palm of my hands became moist I felt my legs being carried away. The excitement had my heart racing out of control and it felt as though it was about to come out of my chest. I put my hand on it in an attempt to soothe the intensity of the beats. I couldn't believe it. It was a yellow canary diamond ring, which had to be at least five carats.

Taj walked over to me, took the ring out of the ice bucket and while never removing his eyes off of me got down on one knee. "Storm, baby, I don't know why you picked somebody like me." Taj nervously licked his lips. "I ain't got no big time degree in philosophy but I got a degree in streetology. It ain't no denying that we gotta bond that's unbreakable. We always gonna be together. No matter what happens in the street we gonna be together. 'Cause I can't circle this life alone – without you. The shit I have worked so hard to build—my club, the houses, my rides—it don't mean nothing to me if I ain't got you sharing it with me. It's all about you. I mean...your real. You a hustler and you know the streets. The streets obey you. But at the same time, you ain't forget how to be a woman, too. I ain't never met a woman that knows how to hold it down on all levels.

'You're my road dawg." Taj put his head down and tried to shake his escalating emotions. "You're my best friend, my happiness...my idol." Then Taj took my left hand, and carefully guided the ring on my finger. "You *define* love...the power to destroy someone but you trust them not to. I love you. And now Storm Williams, I want you to be my wife."

"Oh, my gosh...Taaaaj!"

I had never felt so many good emotions at one time. As far as I was concerned, things couldn't get any better between Taj and me. Yet, I never imagined being his wife. It wasn't that I didn't want to be. And it wasn't that I didn't want to spend a lifetime without him. But I had never allowed myself to fantasize such perfection.

The men that previously had come in and out of my life meant nothing to me. We knew what was up right from the beginning. There were no hidden agendas. They wanted regal pussy and I wanted temporary comfort. I lived by one rule— never let a nigga leave his stain. It always worked—that is—until I meant Taj.

After taking a sip of his drink, Taj said, "We gonna have the biggest mothafuckin' wedding New York ever seen."

"Taj, you want a big wedding?"

"Hell, yeah! We gonna have something so hot even Donald Trump gonna be jealous of it. You know how I do…it's gonna be sick."

I kissed him ravenously. The only time I would drink was when Taj and I were together. Drinking always made me horny. Therefore, I always made sure Taj was around when I did. The alcohol, the realization that I would soon be his wife, Taj's cologne and the heat that was penetrating from his bralic body made me want him more than I ever had before. I anxiously started to unbutton Taj's shirt. "Now let's *really* celebrate and bring this in the right way," I said.

Taj rubbed his hands up and down my butt then gave me a sly smile. "Oh, you being cute, huh?" Then he licked and nibbled on my ear lope. "You sure you ready for this?"

"Mmmm…let me show you," I took his hand and led him to the bedroom.

"You gonna dance for me?"

* * *

The bedroom had floor to ceiling windows. The vertical blinds were dressed in custom burgundy and red drapes. The massive room had a circular bed covered with red stain sheets and a mink comforter, which Taj had covered with rose petals. The room exuded jasmin fragrance, which went along with the ambience. Taj set the magical mood in the room as he took the master remote control instantly the fireplace opened up out of the wall, Brian McKnight was singing *Undeniable* and the lights were dimmed.

CHA-CHING

Taj had the fluke with Cristal and chocolate covered strawberries. We toasted, took a couple of sips and engaged in a long deep kissed. Then he started undressing me, Taj sat on the edge of the bed took both his hands and slowly explored every part of my body as if it were the first time he had laid eyes on it. He carefully laid me down then he took the chocolate covered strawberries out of the fluke and started caressing my body with it. He started from the neck, and then to the tip of my nipples. As he reached the tip, he gently took a bite of the strawberry, and then slowly traced his tongue on my nipple. He continued to lick me until he reached my crown. Then he plunged his tongue inside and skillfully wet my walls. I moaned, gnawed on my bottom lip. I didn't want him to ever stop. I was enjoying the ride he was taking me on. I pushed his head closer to my wet crown.

We continued to take turns kissing, licking, exploring, and caressing each other. Then I got on my knees and stroked his warm and erect muscle. I took my hands and spread his legs open and began softly kissing his inner thighs. Then I ushered his muscle in my mouth and gave him the deluxe oral treatment.

"Daaaaamn baby," Taj screeched and moaned. Not ready to give in to climax, he picked me up and laid me back on the bed. Then he slid his muscle in me. We made love ferociously. We came together, rested and went again. No man had ever had the capabilities of bringing me back a second time...until I met Taj. Finally exhausted we fell asleep.

Suddenly, I felt Taj carefully removing his arm from underneath my head and covering me with the sheets. Then he quietly got out of the bed. I rubbed my eyes attempting to gain focus. "Baby, where you going?" I asked in a whisper.

"I'm 'bout to roll up," he whispered back.

Taj sat on the black swivel recliner. He crushed up his purple haze, laid it out in the blunt and licked one end and twisted up. While he waited for it to dry I poured us another round of drinks. I handed Taj his drink and climbed back into the bed. Taj reached for his torch and fired it up. "You wanna smoke?"

"Yeah," I answered and sat up.

As we were blazing I sat watching Taj. He was fine and *my* man.

Taj walked over to the bed and kissed me on the cheek. "What you thinkin' about?"

"Thinking about us," I said. "The wedding...our life."

"I wanna get married right away."

"Taj!" I purred. "We gotta plan. You say you want a big wedding. I can't plan no wedding overnight."

"You ain't gotta do it yourself. I'll hire somebody. Don't they have people that do that stuff for you?"

"Yeah. They are called wedding planners, baby."

"Right, so that's what we're gonna get. You ain't gotta do nothing yourself. Don't worry about nothing. It's our world, Baby. In 2003 we was sittin' on the mountain top, but in '04 we gonna be dancin' on it!"

Part III

I feel it in the air…

Chapter 11

Our flight back home from Miami had been delayed. A northeastern had slammed eleven inches of snow on top of the gritty streets of New York. After being delayed for two days, Taj and I were finally able to get a flight into Newark Airport.

Rick was waiting for us in Taj's 4.6 Range Rover. He got out of the car and immediately began grabbing our luggage.

"Hey," Rick said, "beautiful weather, huh?"

"Yo, this is crazy. I'm ready to go back to MIA," Taj said.

"Hey, Rick," I said. "Happy New Year!"

Rick and I embraced and then he kissed me on the cheek. "Happy New Year to you, too. Oh, and I heard the good news. That's what's up. Congratulations!"

I felt myself blushing. "Thank you."

Rick anxiously lifted my left hand. "Well, let me see."

I removed my gloves and showed off my ring.

"Damn!"

Taj grinned proudly. "Yo, listen its cold out here. Come on, let's hurry up and get in the truck."

* * *

"Why you keep staring at me, Rick? Don't think I can't see you looking in the rear view mirror."

"Because you look different, Storm. You look happy and peaceful."

"That's 'cause I am."

"Okay, so, when is the wedding?"

"We gonna try and do the joint in April," Taj advised.

"April? That soon?"

"Yeah. And we gonna have a big wedding, too."

"Y'all gonna have to get on the ball then. That's a lot of work."

"I know. It's gonna be all Taj's family and friends. You know I don't have no family and don't really have no friends. If it were up to me we could just go to the Justice of Peace and be done with everything. But this is what Taj want and I want him to have this."

"Taj, you the one that want the big wedding?" Rick asked.

"Yeah, man. Now you know I gotta show off my beautiful wife. Don't no other mothafucka on the planet got a package this tight."

"So, y'all don't want to wait a few more months."

"No," I replied. "We just wanna go on and start with our new life. You know what I'm saying?"

"I hear that. Well, you know I wish y'all nothing but the best. I know y'all gonna make it work. Because you both love each other, power and respect each other. Y'all don't let nothing come in between the two of you. Just keep doing that and you will die old together. I can promise you that."

"Rick, man. You know you gonna have to be my best man."

"For real, man?"

"Of course. Of course. You know that."

"I would be honored, Taj."

"Taj, I just thought of something," I mumbled.

"What?"

"I don't have anybody to walk me down the aisle," I suddenly felt ashamed.

The car instantly grew silent and remained that way for a few minutes.

"You know what? I can do it. I would be more honored to walk you down the aisle, Storm."

"Nah, Rick. You can't do that. I'll figure something out. I don't want you feeling sorry for me. I mean you're Taj's best man."

"Baby, I can have anybody be my best man. Rick should walk you down the aisle."

"Storm, I don't feel sorry for you. Hell, you don't let nobody feel sorry for you. I wanna do this. You know you my baby girl."

"You sure? 'Cause for real, for real, I can walk down the aisle by myself." *I don't really want to do that.*

"I'm positive."

I turned toward Taj and gently held his face in my hands. "You sure you don't mind Taj? We can work something else out."

"I'm sure that I want you to be happy, baby."

"Okay," I placed a gentle kiss on Taj's cheek and rested my head on his chest. *Damn, I love this nigga.*

As if he could read my mind, Taj nibbled on my ear and whispered, "I love you, too, ma."

"Why y'all so quiet back there?"

We both giggled like two school age children. "Nothing," we both sang in unison. I didn't think it was possible to fall deeper in love with Taj but I had.

I looked out the window, besides the snow covered bare trees it didn't look at all like it was a northeastern on the New Jersey Turnpike. "Why is it so much traffic this time of the day?"

"I don't know what's going on," Rick answered.

"Why? You trying to make a stop somewhere before we go home?" Taj asked.

"No. I'm just ready to get home."

"What you gonna wanna eat?"

"I don't know...oh, you know what? I gotta taste for some IHOP."

"IHOP? This time of the day?"

"Uh-huh. You know I can eat pancakes and grits anytime of the day."

"Alright. I guess we can do that. I was hoping for a home cooked meal though. You got some crazy ass eating habits."

"Taj, I don't feel like cooking. Baby, we just got back in town."

"A'ight. I guess I'll just get some Jamaican food from Sonny's. Once we get you straight, I'm gonna check on my moms."

"Okay. You don't want me to come with you?"

"You can come if you want. I ain't bother asking you because you said you were tired. I thought you might just wanna go straight home and get some rest."

"I *am* tired. I'll stop by and see her tomorrow probably."

I put back on my Chanel sunglasses, reached in my Prada handbag for my Mac lip gloss, and then I dabbed my lips. For the remainder of the ride, I daydreamed about my wedding day. I knew I didn't have any family to be there crying and drying their eyes as I walked down the aisle but I really didn't care. Now that Rick was gonna walk me down the aisle, nothing else bothered me. I don't know when it exactly happened but without warning, I suddenly wasn't fearful of committing myself with Taj. Nor was I worried about his commitment to me.

The only worry I had was how I would handle bringing up to Taj where he and I got married. Taj was raised in a strict Pentecostal church, and although he didn't attend church regularly, I knew without a doubt that he would oppose at any suggestions I had of us having our wedding ceremony anywhere but in the church.

* * *

After making all of our food stops, we finally arrived at my apartment.

"Storm, you know you should have on some snow boots or something," Rick said.

"Rick, I'm just leaving Miami. It was 70 degrees when we left there. Do you really think I was thinking about putting on some snow boots when we left there?"

"Well, you knew about the blizzard. You should have told me to bring you some to the airport."

"I'm fine, Rick. Ain't no snow inside the parking garage anyhow."

"Here, Rick, grab that," Taj ordered pointing to my Louis Viutton luggage and garment bag.

"A'ight. I got it. Y'all can go up. I can manage. Madison is probably waiting at the door for you."

"You picked her up from the dog-sitter already?" I asked.

"Yeah, Taj told me to do that this morning when I spoke to him."

Taj and I started walking toward the elevator. "Oh, Storm, I know what I forgot to tell you. That crazy ass Pam been blowing up my phone looking for you."

"What for?"

"She said you ain't been returning her calls."

"She's right and her ass know I was out of town with my man so I don't know why she keep calling."

"I don't know either."

"When the last time she called?"

"She called about seven o'clock this morning."

"Seven o'clock?

"Uh-huh."

"Well, what she be saying?"

"Oh, she was just talking a whole lot of bullshit about you ain't been talking to her and she don't know what's up with you. And she hope you ain't tryin' to play her?"

"She said that?" Taj asked.

"Yeah, man. She's been acting like she's maniac or something."

"You told her I was coming back today?"

"Nah, but if I'm not mistaken, I think she knew that already."

"How she know that though? I didn't tell her when I was coming back. Why is the bitch sweating me like that? You wait until I call her psychotic triflin' ass."

Taj held the "Door Open" button on the elevator while Rick pulled the luggage in.

"Don't worry about it," Taj assured. "Just handle your business and then be done with it."

"You know I'm gonna handle her. But I'm saying though...what's that all about? I mean why the hell is that stupid bitch calling Rick looking for me? She act like we be eating each other pussies or something. I don't like that shit. When I'm ready to talk to her, I'll call her. That's why the bitch is cut-off 'cause she on some stupid shit right now and I don't have time for that."

"Maybe she know about the Crimesolvers thing and that's why she trying to get at you," Rick replied.

"I don't care…she still don't need to be running me down for that. That shit is on her. I ain't tell her to walk up in that store all open like that. She know I trained her betta than that."

* * *

When we walked into the apartment, Madison came running out of my bedroom. I hugged and played with her for a few minutes. Then I took off my Jimmy Choo boots and collapsed on the sofa. Rosa had retrieved all the mail and left it on the sofa table. I reached for the latest edition of *Essence* magazine; Queen Latifah was on the cover. I glanced through some of the pages then put the magazine down.

Taj turned on the television then went into the kitchen to warm up our food.

"Baby, what you want to drink with this?"

"Do we have any juice?"

"No."

"Well, I guess I'll just drink some milk then."

"Storm, this milk is old."

"I told Rosa's ass to buy some milk. See what I'm saying?"

"Calm down baby. I'll go get you some milk if you want some that bad."

"That's alright. I don't want you to have to go back out. Go on and eat. I know you are hungry."

"Why you seem so stressed since we got back? Is that shit about Pam bothering you?"

"I guess it is." Then my cell phone began to ring. It was Pam.

"That's her?"

"Yup."

"Answer it and get it over with."

"No, I don't feel like dealing with her right now. When I'm ready to talk, I'll call her. She ain't gonna *make* me talk to her."

"Well, stop stressing it then. After you eat I'm gonna run your water so you can take a bath. And while I'm at my moms I want you to relax and get yourself together. Remember we got a wedding we need to start planning for."

I smiled at the reminder and stretched out my hand to admire my engagement ring. "Thanks, boo."

Taj handed me my plate of food. "Here, go on and eat."

* * *

Taj had decided to take Madison along for the ride to visit his mother. The warm bubble bath and listening to Maxwell was definitely what I needed to relax me. I grabbed a Heineken from the refrigerator and rolled up a blunt to finish me off. As I waited for the blunt to dry, the telephone rang again...it was Pam. *Damn what the fuck is her problem?*

"Hello," I said in an irritated tone.

"Storm?"

"What?"

"Well, damn. Where the hell you been? Why you ain't been returning any of my calls?"

"I ain't know I had to check in with you. My bad."

"What's that all about?"

"What?"

"The attitude. I mean if you got something to say then I would appreciate it if you would be woman enough to say it."

Did this bitch just have the audacity to challenge my womanhood? "Oh, you know I'm definitely woman enough to say what the fuck is on my mind. Pam, you of all people should know that by now."

"Alright, then. What's up?"

"I'm not getting into this because you feel like you need to know right now. I told you I'm tired. I just got back from my trip with my fiancé—"

Pam quickly interrupted me. "Fiancé?"

"Yeah."

"So, you and Taj are getting married?"

"We sure are."

"Well, why you ain't tell me that before? When did all this happen? Why you acting so secretive, Storm? I mean you didn't even call a bitch and say Happy New Year or nothing. What's up with that? I thought you was my dog."

Just listening to her speak was beginning to annoy me. "Listen, are you done?"

"Am I done? Am I done?" Pam repeated, her voice began to escalate in anger. "Storm, is that what you just asked me?"

"Pam, I ain't stutter. And I'm not gonna say it again, I'm tired. I'll call you tomorrow." Then I put the receiver down.

CHA-CHING

I waited a few minutes to see if Pam would call back. She didn't. *Good.* Then I pulled back the black mink bedspread, climbed into the bed and began to light up.

* * *

I flicked the television channels until I got to *Cribs*. Kimora Lee and Russell Simmons were showcasing their New Jersey mansion. *Maybe Taj and I could rent out a mansion for the wedding. Yeah, now that might work. Taj is gaudy. Now if anything, he will go for that idea over a church. I'm almost positive he will. He has been after me to start looking at mansions in Jersey anyway. Yeah, that's how I'm gonna approach it. We can BUY the mansion and have the wedding there. Taj loves to show off, he'll definitely go for it.*

My eyelids became heavy and trying to keep them open became a chore. Finally, I gave in to sleep and resigned to analyze my wedding plans after my nap.

* * *

Taj and I was in Jamaica. The weather was beautiful. We were walking barefoot on the sand. I was dressed in an ivory Vera Wang ankle length dress and Taj had on ivory pants, and shirt. His shirt was only buttoned at the bottom.

Rick was bellowing, Kenny Lattimore's, *You* and Taj and I were dancing. We were smiling and laughing. There were a few people circled around us, admiring our love. Yet, we were oblivious to them. It was as if we were the only two people in the world.

After Rick finished singing, Rick and all of the spectators left quickly. Taj picked me up and gently cradled me like a newborn baby. We kissed passionately. Then he laid me on the sand. White candles surrounded us. They were everywhere-- hundreds of them. Despite the breeze, the candles remained lit. It was so serene and peaceful. The only thing you heard was the music from the sea. My heart was flooded with joy.

Taj and I fondled each other, kissed and made love. We rested, then, I turned to him and looked him in his eyes and said, "Thank you for bringing me here. You know I love the sea."

Taj just smiled. Then I climbed on top of him and slowly eased his penis in me. I moved up and down, side to side, slow then fast--just the way I knew Taj loved it. Taj had his mouth slightly opened, his head titled and eyes rolling to the back of his head. He was obviously enjoying the ride that I was taking him on. Watching Taj turned me on more than I could have imagined that it could. I felt like my walls were going to collapse and started going faster and faster...

The telephone rang and woke me out of my sleep. I had been humping the bed. *Damn.*

"Hello," I answered in a sleep raspy voice.

"Hey, baby," Taj answered. "I'm sorry. I didn't want to wake you up. Just was checking on you."

"No, it's okay," I assured rubbing the sleep from my eyes. "I'm good. When you coming home?"

"I'm still at my moms. I should be home in about two hours."

"Two hours, Taj?"

"Yeah. What's wrong?"

I sighed. "You know I was just humping the bed?"

"What?"

"I had a dream that we was in Bahamas or it may have been Jamaica. I think we had gotten married there. And Rick was there singing at the wedding."

"You know Rick could blow?"

"No. Rick can sing?"

"Yeah."

"Shit. This is wild."

"So you were humping the bed Storm?"

I laughed a little embarrassed at the thought. "Yeah. After, I guess the wedding, you and I was on the beach and we starting making love and the shit must've been good 'cause I was humping the bed."

Taj laughed. "Well, I promise I'll take care of you when I get home."

"Alright. I wondered what made me dream we were at the beach. I don't never dream."

"You love the sea and the water. That's probably why. And you always dream, Storm. You probably just don't remember your dreams."

"Oh, well, tell your moms hi. And even if I'm sleep when you get home, make sure you wake me up."

"Okay. Now remember you said that."

"I'm serious. Make sure that you wake me up, Taj."

"You know how hard that is."

"It won't be hard tonight. I promise."

"Well, just sleep with your legs open."

"Cute. See you later, baby."

"A'ight," Taj chuckled. "Later."

The telephone rang again. It was Pam. *This bitch is begging for me to curse her ass out.*

"Hello," I snapped.

"Hey, Storm."

"What you want Pam? I told you I was tired and I would talk to you tomorrow. I mean why you bugging?"

"I'm not bugging. But I don't appreciate the way you treating me. I mean one minute we are the best of friends and the next minute you acting like I done cross you or something."

"Pam, trust me, if you had crossed me you wouldn't be on this phone talking to me."

"Really?"

"Oh, that's real."

"Well, I'm not gonna *bother* you no more. I was just calling you because I had some paper to give to you."

"What paper?"

"Trez gave me the money he owed you."

"Oh, really? What made him finally do that all of the sudden?"

"I told him that you was gonna send Taj after him if he didn't pay up."

"You told him that?"

"Yeah."

"Pam, you know I don't like throwing Taj's name out there for the benefit of my business. I run the streets on my name, not Taj's."

"I know that but I really wanted to get the money from Trez. I thought that that was why you were mad at me."

"I ain't mad at you."

"So are you gonna tell me or what?"

"I told you...we can talk tomorrow."

"Well, we gonna have to talk over the phone then because I gotta leave town tomorrow."

"Oh, yeah. Where you going?"

"I gotta go and check on my grandmother. She's been sick and you know how my people are? Ain't nobody trying to take care of her they just taking her money and shit. So I gotta go and take care of that. And...and I don't know when I'm coming back."

Something is up. She must've forgotten who she talking to 'cause this bitch don't give a damn about her grandmother. "I hear that. Well we can get together when you get back then."

"Storm, you gonna want me to carry that money around with me?"

"Yeah, it's good. You can give it to me when you get back."

Pam sighed. "A'ight. One."

"Okay, talk to you later."

I pressed the receiver down so I could get a dial tone and call Taj. I started dialing his cell number and decided it could wait. I didn't want him to think I was still trippin' over Pam.

* * *

After I hung up the telephone, I laid back down and tried to fall back asleep. A half hour later the intercom rang.

"Yeah."

"Good evening, Ms. Williams. Miss Pam is here to see you."

Pam? I paused for a few moments. "Alright, you can send her up."

Five minutes went by and Pam still had not arrived at my apartment. I picked up the phone and dialed the doorman. "Hi, this is Ms. Williams. My guest never made it to my apartment. Did she leave?"

"No, Ms. Williams. Miss Pam and the other two young ladies went up a few minutes ago. I saw them get on the elevator."

"Two other young ladies?"

"Yes, she had two women with her."

"Why you didn't say that before?" Then the doorbell rang. "Hold up. That's her now. Okay, bye."

When I opened up the door, only Pam was standing there. She was dressed all thugged out with Rocawear velour jogging suit and field Tims. "What's up with you?" I asked.

"Nothing," Pam said nervously.

"Nothing. Well, why you here? I told you I wasn't stressing the money. In fact, I told you about ten times, I was tired. Why you acting like you on crack or something?" Then I pushed her to the side and stuck my head the door, where are them bitches that came here with you?"

"What you talking about?"

"My doorman said you were with two other chicks. Where are they?"

"Oh, them. I used to go to school with with..." Pam stammered, "One of them and the other one you know her she um...that's Aja, that video bitch."

"You don't seem to be doing too well in the hearing department today. I ain't ask you who they were. I ask you where the fuck are they?"

"I don't know, Storm. They went to see somebody on the eighteenth floor."

"Oh, yeah?"

"Yeah, now can I come in? Damn?"

I opened the door and Pam walked in. I stood and watched her as she unfastened her coat.

"Where Madison?"

"She ain't here. Why you wanna know?"

"I just asked for her that's all. I thought it was quiet when we was on the phone."

"So, why are you here?"

Pam threw her hands in the air. "I'm so stressed, Storm. I got so much drama going on with my family and shit. I just needed to talk to you. When I called you I was only five minutes away and I wasn't gonna come up after you told me to wait until I got back to give you the money but I really needed to talk to you."

"Which one is it?"

"What?"

"On one hand, you really needed to give me the money that Trez gave you for me. Which by the way, you have been in my apartment about five minutes or more....if you had the money you should've handed it to me before you stepped foot in my house. I mean, if that's why you here. Then on the next hand, you stressed about your grandmother. The same grandmother that you have repeatedly told me you can't stand."

"When have I ever told you I can't stand my grandmother, Storm?"

"Many times."

"Name one time I ever said that shit out my mouth Storm?"

"Listen, I ain't gonna go back and forth with this juvenile shit. I let you in, even after I told you I didn't want to see or talk to you. So tell me what's up? And make it fast, 'cause I'm not feeling this at all right now."

"Storm, why you treating me like this? Why you treating me like I'm a stranger or something. I thought we were family."

"I don't have no family."

"You know what I mean. You acting so distant with me. Like I done threw some dirt on you and shit. I never thought you of all people would turn on me like this. After all we done been through. I mean for real, for real, I turned you on to the game. And this is how you gonna do me?"

I ignored Pam's rhetoric. "So you here to talk about the same thing I said could wait until you came back? That's what's stressing you?"

"Yeah, part of it."

"So why you lie, Pam. Why you come all the way here to lie in my face?"

"I mean, my grandmother *is* sick."

"I don't want to talk about your grandmother or anybody else. You obviously don't have my money and you already know it's all about the Cha-Ching. So you need to go."

CHA-CHING

"Storm!"

"What? Why the hell you screaming out my name like that in my damn house?"

"Storm, I'm not leaving here until you tell me what's up with you? I mean all of the sudden you getting married and shit. Just the other day, you and Taj couldn't stand each other. Y'all could of had y'all own reality show and shit and now look you getting married and walking around flashing that big mothafucking ring like it's all good. I'm tired of you walking around here thinking your shit don't stink 'cause you can stand on top of your wallet and shit. You ain't betta that the next bitch."

"Hold up!" I opened up the door. "Bitch, get the fuck out of my house before I whip your ass. You must be crazy...or on some serious shit to think you can come up on some hatarade bullshit in my fucking house and talk shit to me. Get out! Bitch I said get the fuck out!"

Pam slowly got up from the sofa. Then she started putting on her coat.

"Put that bitch on when you leave here, get out now!"

When Pam got to the door, she stopped in the doorway and just stared at me.

"What?" I pointed my index finger on her forehead. "You don't scare me Pam. Don't play with me."

"Yo," Pam looked around the hallway from side to side.

"What is that suppose to do?"

"YO!"

I pushed the door to force Pam's foot out of the doorway. Then everything began to move in slow motion. Pam pushed the door open and stomped on my foot. Then two other chicks ran from around the corner. Pam had a large black object in her hand and in less than a minute I felt severe pain all over my face. "Cha-Ching this bitch!" Pam yelled. I fell to the floor. Pam continued to hit me with the large object. I could no longer see. All I could think about doing was trying to crawl to where I kept my nine mila. But I couldn't even move. I felt blood profusely escaping from my mouth. My body was numb. I occasionally felt a foot kick me here and there. I tried to call out to Taj, but I couldn't speak. All I could do was moan.

Chapter 12

The next morning, the *New York Post* newspaper headlines read: BEAUTY SAVAGELY BEATEN AND LEFT FOR DEAD. COPS SUSPECT DRUG DEAL GONE BAD.

After I laid in a pool of my own blood for more than two hours, Taj had finally came home and discovered the gruesome scene in which Pam and her chicks had left me. I was taken to New York University Hospital and was immediately taken into surgery. I spent almost six hours in the operating room.

Envy, greed and deception had left me clinging to life with four broken ribs; a broken pelvic; a cracked skull; my nose had been crushed; I had lost eight teeth, lost hearing in my left ear and lost my eye sight. The doctor's informed told Taj that is was a miracle that I was alive and that they didn't expect me to make it through the surgery. But I had. I was fighting.

I was fighting for the life that was ahead with Taj. Fighting for another opportunity to say "I love you," and fighting to hug Madison. There was no way that fate had this planned for me. I could not accept that without any warning, I had so quickly and violently approached the end of my road.

* * *

For the first five days Taj never left my bedside. He wouldn't let the nurses bathe me. He did that. He had developed a routine, he would start the day brushing my hair, then he would lotion my body, massage my legs, and at least three times a day he would change my socks. Then, he would put on the cartoons. When *Jimmy Neutron* came on he would always turn up the volume. I don't know why, but I loved watching *Jimmy Neutron*. Before I got hurt, sometimes out of the blue I would walk up to Taj and say, "Gotta blast!" He would always laugh and say, "Yeah, I gotta go. Storm, you know you crazy right?"

Rick, Rosa and Taj's mother would occasionally come to visit and to relieve him, but he would always refuse to leave. Although I was unconscious and I couldn't speak to Taj, I could hear him speak to me. He didn't know it, but his words, his presence, and his love wrapped around me like a warm blanket and comforted me.

At the end of the day, Taj would read me an article out of one of my favorite magazines. Then he would play my favorite music. Sometimes he would put Jay Z and Beyoncé', *Bonnie & Clyde* on repeat. Taj and I often referred to that song as *our* anthem. On the outside I am sure that he appeared to be holding it down.

He had a bodyguard placed outside of my hospital room twenty-four hours a day. Taj had the streets on lockdown and within two hours of finding me and ultimately discovering that Pam had committed that violation against me, he ordered a hit on her. Less than twenty-two hours later, Pam was found dead in a dumpster on Bushwick Avenue in Brooklyn. Every bone in her body had been broken.

* * *

Like I said, on the outside Taj was in control. Nothing scared him. Yet, on the inside my man was falling apart.

Taj reached for my hand and held it tightly. Then he began to cry. I wanted desperately to hold him and tell him that I was going to be okay. I wanted to remind him of my past, on how much turmoil and pain that I had already overcame. Even though I was only 125 pounds, I was strong and I was gonna make it. *We* were gonna make it.

Suddenly, I could feel my breathing becoming shallow. Although I was very young when I lived with my mother, I still vividly remember her explaining to me what happens to your body when you are about to die. I remember because I was always intrigued with the passage of death...intrigued because I didn't understand why and how.

I felt Taj come closer to me. Then he began to speak to me. He started off in a whisper. "Baby, it's alright. I know what you're doing. I know you trying to hold on for me—for us," Taj paused and I could hear him lick his lips, the way he always did when he was bothered, nervous or sad. "Oh, man. I can't believe this shit. But it's alright. I'm gonna be okay. I promise, I'll take care of myself and you know you don't have to worry about Madison. I'll take care of her." Taj broke down crying like a newborn baby. "Storm, baby, I love you. I'm gonna always love you, Storm. I never ever loved anyone the way that I love you. I don't know why…I don't know why God is taking you from me right now. And I ain't gonna ever understand why you had to suffer like this, baby. But, uh…but…I…I know I gotta let you go.

"Everybody…everybody keep telling me that you are holding on for me. You know what I'm saying? And I…I…I need to let you know that it's okay…that *I'm* okay. That our dreams, and our love it don't end here. It doesn't end like this. We gonna finish this, boo. We gonna finish, I can promise you that. You know, I don't ever start something and don't finish it.

"I know you don't believe in the other side, but I hope and pray to God that over the past week you have made some kinda peace with God. You gotta make peace with God so that we can be together. Storm, you gotta forgive, so that we can finish what we have. I've accepted that we gonna have to finish it in Heaven. And no, it's not how I wanted it and boo, you know I hate it when I'm not in control, but I'll take anything…anything just as long as I can be with you."

I wanted to tell Taj, I was fighting back. I couldn't leave him like this. I couldn't leave him wondering. I wanted so badly to be in his arms. In his arms is where I felt safe.

I tried to move my hands. I couldn't. Then I tried to just move one finger. I concentrated on the finger that he was rubbing—my index finger.

"Baby, you hear me? You hear me don't you? I knew it! I knew you could hear me. Boo, if you can hear me, move your finger again? Come on ma, you can do it. I know you can do it."

I decided to concentrate on the index finger once again. Slowly I was able to move it again.

"Storm," Taj cried out ecstatically.

The joy in his voice made me feel that at the moment I could do anything. I immediately commanded my body to sit up, move, walk, and jump. Nothing happened. So I decided to focus on one thing at a time. I realized I had to take it slow. I began to focus on opening my eyes. I felt them open slow—very slow. Then they closed. Then they opened again. But I couldn't see. No matter which direction that I moved my eyeballs, I only saw total blackness. I panicked and wanted to tell Taj. I had to tell Taj that I couldn't see.

I tried to speak but I was unable--there was a large tube in my mouth. I turned my focus once again on my hands. Somehow, I had to gain the strength to move my hand. I needed to tell Taj to take that tube out of my mouth. I needed to tell him that even though my eyes were open, I couldn't see him.

"Storm," Taj sniffled. "I'm here," he added. "I'm right here, baby." Suddenly, I heard footsteps. Someone had walked into my hospital room. From the sound of the heels, it was a woman—an overweight woman.

The room smelled like a florist. There were roses to the left of me and to my right there must have been an exotic arrangement and somewhere nearby in the room there was eucalyptus. There may have even been a few stems placed in the exotic arrangement. Right above my head, I heard the sound of a fluorescent light hum and steady flicker. Next to the roses, I heard a machine beep then pause, then beep again.

I also heard noises coming from the doorway. Some were stronger than the others. There were people walking by, machines beeping, and telephones were constantly ringing. I was already teaching my right ear to become my eyes.

The woman had walked to where Taj stood and I could feel her presence at the foot of my bed. "My wife just spoke. Get a doctor in here right now. RIGHT NOW!" I heard her heels quickly click and clatter away, until they faded with the rest of the noise, and blended with the hustle and bustle in the hospital corridor.

* * *

It had been four days since I had been taken off of the respirator. I had developed an infection and ran a fever for almost two straight days. It appeared that I wasn't going to make it through this battle. I would put my foot inside death's door, but something or someone kept me from giving up and walking all the way in.

I smelled candles burning--my favorite, vanillaroma and peaches and cream scented. The room was so peaceful. I knew Taj was there but he didn't speak to me. *Maybe he is sleep. Just let him sleep, Storm.* He must have read my mind. "I'm not sleep. I was just laying here watching how beautiful you are."

"Laying?" I asked.

Taj chuckled. "Yeah, the nurses got me a cot. I guess they saw I wasn't trying to go anywhere, so they bought this in to me earlier this afternoon."

"Oh, baby. I'm so sorry. I want you to go home tonight and get a good night's rest. You ain't gonna be no good for me, if you don't get any rest."

I heard the cot creek, then Taj's bare feet walking toward me. "As long as you have to sleep in here, I'm gonna sleep here and be with you. I'm not gonna leave you, Storm. I don't care what...I'm never gonna leave you." His last words seem to be speaking of something deeper than just leaving me in the hospital alone.

"What about the club though? You know if niggas don't see you they start thinking you getting weak on them."

"I've been checking on the club. Everything is fine. I went by there last night. Don't worry about nothing, Storm. I got everything under control. Just take care of you. Concentrate on getting yourself stronger so you can get out of here and go home. Madison is missing you."

"Ah...and I miss her, too. I just wanna hug her." I started to fight back my tears.

"It's okay," Taj reassured.

"Taj?" I whispered.

"Yeah."

"Can you please lay next to me?"

"Of course."

First, Taj walked over to the CD and pressed play. *Bonnie & Clyde*, started to play. Then he climbed into the bed, gently he lifted me up and placed my body close to his. In my mind, I could picture him so clearly. His perfect smile, and his beautiful brown skin. Slowly Taj glided, and then I glided. I cried, and then he cried. He sang and then he rocked until I fell asleep.

* * *

The next morning, Taj did his daily morning routine. Once he was done, Taj told me that he had to take care of a few things. A few minutes later Rick came in and relieved Taj.

"Hey, baby girl. How you feeling today?" Rick asked.

"I'm okay." I grunted, "I'm just a little sore today."

"Have you taken your medicine already?"

"Uh-huh."

"Good. Can they give you anything for the soreness?"

"I don't know. I'll be okay. Maybe it's the way I slept last night. I would do anything for a nice warm bubble bath."

I heard Rick fumbling with a plastic bag. I smelled fried chicken.

"What's that? Is that KFC you eating?"

"Nah, Popeye's. I couldn't find any KFC near here."

"Oh."

"Oh, my bad. You want some? They still got you on that liquid diet don't they?"

"No. I can eat solid food now. But no, I don't want none. Taj and I ate breakfast not too long ago. What time is it? Ain't it too early to be eating lunch?"

"It's 11:30. You know I don't eat breakfast though."

"Oh, that's right. I forgot that."

"I'm sorry, Storm."

"Nah, it's okay. You don't have to keep apologizing Rick. It ain't your fault that this has happened to me. You can't help that I have trouble remembering things. I'm getting better though."

"I know. I'm proud of you, you know that right? I know you a fighter though."

"I don't know about that. How is Taj doing Rick?"

"He's fine, Storm. You know he can take care of himself. Don't worry about Taj. Just worry about getting betta, baby. That's all."

"I gotta worry about him. I don't want him running himself raggedy. He don't deserve this. He don't deserve having to worry about taking care of me...spending the rest of his life taking care of a blind woman that he probably get sick to his stomach looking at anyway."

"Girl, what are you talking about?"

"I'm talking about the way I look. I can feel my face. I may not be able to see it, but I can feel it. It feels ugly."

"Storm, you still the same beautiful woman you were before the accident. The only thing that is different about you is right now you can't see. That's it."

I knew he was telling a lie. But his lie comforted me. "Right now? Forever you mean? For the rest of my life?"

"You can't say that Storm. I mean look at you. The doctors didn't expect you to make it through the surgery. You a fighter. You gonna defy all the odds—believe me. And before you know it, you gonna be your old self again. Driving everybody crazy. Cursing everybody out. And then, when you are all betta, you and Taj gonna get married."

"I hope so."

"I know so. And when you do, I'm gonna sing at the wedding."

"I'm gonna hold you to that."

Amidst the hustle, and the noise in the hospital corridor, I heard a different walk, I smelled a different scent.

"Is that--"

Madison came running into my room, licking me, crying and barking. Taj walked over to my bedside and lifted me up. Madison jumped on the bed.

"Taj, how did you manage to bring her in here?"

"You know I can make things happen. Especially when it come to you."

I played with Madison for almost fifteen minutes. Then we said our goodbyes and Rick took her back home.

* * *

"Thank you, Taj. I can't believe you managed to get Madison up in here like that."

"No problem, baby. You know I would do anything for you."

"You know sometimes I get so angry because I don't understand why this had to happen to me. But then I look at you, you are unbelievable. There is no other man that can even stand next to you. I'm so proud of you. I don't have many good men to compare you to but I know that they don't make men like you."

"Storm, ain't nothing I'm doing that the next man wouldn't do for you. You make a nigga just wanna hand you the world. You do it to me. You bring out the best of me."

I suddenly became quiet. "Taj?"

"Yes, Storm."

"I'm scared."

"I know. I know you are, ma."

"Taj?"

"Yes, Storm."

"Am I still pretty?"

Taj kissed me on the cheek and worked his way to my lips. "Storm Williams, you are beautiful."

* * *

In the middle of the night, I heard the cot squeaking. Taj would get up and walk back and forth. I would hear him typing on his two-way. Then he would take the remote control and flick through the channels. I had been suffering with a headache the entire day. The pain medication had me pretty groggy but I had to shake out of it and find out what was bothering Taj.

"Taj," I whispered softly.

"Yeah, Storm. What's the matter? You in pain or something?"

"No, I'm okay."

"You gotta go to the bathroom? You need me to bring your bed pan? You want some cold water?"

"No. What's the matter with you?"

"With *me*?"

"Yeah."

"Nothing. Ain't nothing wrong with me. Why you say that?"

"I hear you, Taj. I hear you walking, pacing, twisting and turning. I know you. What's wrong?"

"I just can't sleep."

"Why?"

"I don't know. It bothers me watching you suffer like this. I mean, you cried all day because of those damn headaches. Yo, I hate this. I hate not being able to make this betta. I feel like a failure because not only wasn't I there to protect you...to stop this from happening to you, I can't take away your pain. It's hard, Storm. I hate watching you going through this...if it's not the headaches, it's the fever. If it's not the fevers, it's the infection. Why?"

"I'm sorry."

"I'm sorry, Storm. My bad. I shouldn't be acting like this."

"You are only human, Taj. You need to let out your frustration, too. It's not good to keep everything in. Stop worrying. I'm gonna be fine and then I'm gonna be able to take care of you. Come here, hold my hand."

"Um...I was thinking."

"About what?"

"Don't get mad at me for bringing this up. I'm just gonna throw it out there...you don't have to agree with me or nothing like that."

"What, Taj?" I asked concerned.

"Why don't you let me look and see if I can find your mother or something?"

"My mother? Why the hell did you bring her up? My mother is probably dead somewhere."

"You don't know that Storm."

"You right, I don't know that. I don't care to know either. If she ain't dead. She might as well be."

"I didn't bring it up to upset you. I just thought that maybe now was the time you needed her. Maybe you need to talk to her."

"Taj, I appreciate you. I appreciate you looking out for me and standing by me and everything but I don't need my mother. I needed my mother years ago. I needed my mother when I was sucking dicks just to eat. That's when I needed my mother. Yeah, I needed my mother when I stole food to eat; when I had to eat raw spaghetti for breakfast and vanilla frosting for dinner. That's when I needed my mother. The only thing I need right now is to see again. That's it. You are my mother, my father, my man, my world. I don't need that part of my life back."

"I'm just saying. I just feel bad."

"Taj, feel bad about what? That I don't have no family coming to visit me?"

"Yeah."

"But I do. You are my family, Rick is my family, Rosa...well, Rosa is my family when she ain't getting on my damn nerves." We both chuckled.

"You sure, Storm?"

"I'm positive. I'm fine."

"Sometimes I just feel so helpless."

"Taj you are what brought me back from death's door. Don't you know that? How can you sit there and say that?"

"Storm, you always have a way of making me feel like I can conquer the world."

I heard rain tapping at the windows. "Is that rain?"

"Yes, it's suppose to rain for the next three days."

"I hate it when it rains."

"I know you do. I always think of you and smile when it rains. Because I know how much you always fuss when it does rain."

"Taj, can you carry me to the window?"

"Huh? What for?"

"Please."

"Storm, you know betta."

"Taj, I'll be fine."

"Why? You don't like the rain. We just finished talking about that."

"I know. But for some reason, I wanna be close to the outdoors. You know I love the outdoors. Especially when it's hot out."

Taj let the guardrail carefully down, wrapped me in the blanket and then he carried me next to the window and sat me on his lap.

I placed my hand on the window. I could feel the cold. I could feel the water hit the glass. The window would faintly vibrate each time the rain hit it.

"What are you thinking about?"

"I'm thinking about the beach, the sun, and the sand."

"Do you remember telling me that you had a dream that we were married on the beach?"

"No."

"You don't remember telling me that you dreamt that we had gotten married on the beach and that Rick had sung for us?"

"No. That's funny you said that 'cause he told me today that he is gonna sing for our wedding. I didn't even know that Rick could even sing."

"That's what you said when you told me about the dream and I told you he could sing."

"Did you tell him about the dream?"

"Yeah, when you first got hurt I told him."

"Oh, then that's why he said that. Taj?"

"Yeah, ma."

"If you still wanna marry me—"

"What you mean *if* I still wanna marry you? Why you talking crazy?"

"I mean, it's not crazy. I can't see. Do you wanna spend the rest of your life with a woman that can't take care of herself?"

"I'm not gonna spend the rest of my life with a woman that can't take care of herself. You know why? Because this situation right here is temporary. You ain't gonna always be this way. I give you my word—"

I interrupted him. "How can you give me your word on that?"

"Because I can, that's how. I give you my word that one day you will see again."

"Taj please don't tell me that. There is no way you can guarantee me that."

"Let's stop talking about it. Are you ready to get back in the bed?"

"No, not yet. Just a few more minutes then I'll be ready."

"Okay."

"Taj, I hope that you are right. 'Cause I don't like the darkness. I don't want to spend the rest of my life like this. I don't wanna die. But I don't wanna live without being free." Then Taj held me tightly.

"We gonna beat this."

"Taj, you ever thought about having kids?"

"Yeah, I used to think of it sometime. But I know you wasn't ready for that, so I don't bring it up. I mean you said you don't like kids."

"You can't always keep your dreams a secret to make me happy."

"Well, one day, I guess when you are ready I planned on bringing it up."

"I want a child. Maybe we can have two kids. I want two boys. Because the world deserves more men like you."

Chapter 13

Three weeks had passed by since my accident. Everyday presented itself with a new challenge. One day, I was wiggling my toes, seeing white flashes and the next day I was screaming because of the headaches. Taj and I were on an emotional rollercoaster. One I was definitely ready to get off of.

For the past couple of days, I had been having a steady visitor—Lisa Santana. Lisa had read about me in the newspapers. Lisa was from Richmond, Virginia and had come to New York to work on a documentary about female hustlers and wanted to know more about me. I resisted her initially, but it was something about her that was different—genuine. I barely opened up myself to strangers, but despite my initial resistance I had opened myself up to Lisa. I could sense that Taj was pleased that we had hit it off. Maybe I did it for him.

No matter how mean I was to Lisa she came back the next day. I had a feeling that she could relate to me more than she had led on. In the beginning, I would hear her writing down notes, but I didn't hear that anymore. Now it seemed that she had what she needed for the documentary. But she still kept coming back.

"Boo, you sure you don't want no more eggs?" Taj asked.

"No, I'm full."

"Okay."

"Taj, can you lift up the bed a little bit for me?"

"Sure," Taj pressed on the button. "Is this good enough?"

"Yes, that's fine. Thank you."

"I spoke to Rosa and she was gonna go ahead and make the appointment for you to get your hair done. But I told her to hold off on that 'cause you wasn't doing so good yesterday."

"Yeah. That's fine. I don't think I'm up to that just yet. Does it look bad?"

"No."

"The braids don't look old? They feel old?"

"Nah, baby. It looks good. You know I wouldn't lie to you."

"I can't wait to get a fresh dubie."

"Soon you will be able to. Real soon."

I started to cough. "Taj pass me some tissue please?"

"You need to sit up a little bit." He started feeling my forehead. "Damn."

"What's wrong?"

"I think you running a fever again. Let me go and get the nurse to check your temperature. I'll be right back."

As Taj was walking out of the room, I heard footsteps—a woman's footsteps walking in the room. Her scent was familiar. The perfume she wore was familiar. It was soft and light. It reminded me of my mother. My heart began to race. "Who is that? Who just came in?"

The steps came closer. "Hi, Storm. It's me, Lisa."

"Oh."

"Well, gee whiz."

"I'm sorry."

"Is something wrong?"

"No, you have on different perfume today."

"Oh, I didn't realize you recognized that."

"I have to. I like to know who is in my presence."

"Well, actually, I do have on something different today. It's Windsong. I used to wear it a lot but I have a hard time finding it in Richmond."

"Windsong? I think my mother used to wear that."

"Oh, really."

"Yeah."

"Well, how are you feeling today?"

"A little betta…I guess."

"How is the coughing?"

"I'm not coughing as much. Well, at night I seem to cough so much."

"Do you think that it is too cold in here during the night?"

"No."

I heard Lisa pulled her chair closer to the bed.

"Why are you staring at me?"

"How do you know that I'm staring at you?"

"I can feel it. Besides, your silence tells me that you are."

"It's amazing how you have learned to have you ear see for you in such a short time. Have you had a therapist work with you?"

"No."

"I'm surprised."

"I don't need no therapist. All I need is to see again. That's it. I'm tired of being in this hospital. I'm tired of being in this bed. I'm tired of coughing...tired of everything."

Taj walked back into the room with the nurse. I hated the daytime shift and was hoping she wasn't going to come at me all rough, because I was gonna curse her out if she did.

"Yes, her temperature is up. I'll let her doctor know."

Taj poured me some water. "Here, boo, drink some water. We gotta get that temperature down again."

I took a few sips. "That's it. I'll drink some more later.

"Maybe you need some rest."

"Well, I can go. I think rest is probably what you need too Storm," Lisa agreed.

"Nah, it's okay. You can stay," Taj said.

"Taj, I'm really not tired. I thought you had to run a few errands."

"I do. But I'm not going nowhere until the doctor comes and checks you."

"I can wait here until you get back," Lisa offered.

"You sure?"

"Yes, I don't mind."

"Oh, okay. Thanks. Here, let me write down my cell phone number just in case you need to get in touch with me."

"Okay. I'll promise that I'll call you right away if anything should come up."

"A'ight. Make sure that they give her some Tylenol or something to help bring down that fever. Sometimes these nurses on the daytime shift get lazy and shit and you gotta stay on them."

"Definitely. Don't worry about it. I got it."

Taj kissed me on the forehead and then he left.

"How is the weather?"

"It's not too bad out today. Not as cold out as it was yesterday. I think it's gonna go up to the thirty's today?"

"That's what I don't miss. I can't stand the cold."

"Oh, no. That's strange. With a name like Storm you would think you love the cold weather."

"Everybody always say that. So tell me, how is your documentary thing going?"

"It's going good. I think I just have one more young lady that I need to interview and then I'm done."

"Who is the chick you need to interview?"

"Um...I don't know her name off hand."

At my request, Lisa turned on the radio. Hot 97 was playing and Angie Martinez was talking about a Valentine's day concert featuring: Jill Scott, Musiq, and a few other artists whose name that I didn't catch.

"Valentine's day is coming already."

"I know. These holidays just come and go so quickly. I'm telling you. It seemed like it was just Christmas the other day," Lisa agreed.

"You know this Christmas was the first Christmas that I had celebrated since I was a little girl."

"Really?" Lisa seemed hesitant to ask why. "Why?"

"Just a lot of reasons. I don't even know why I brought that up."

"You brought it up because you wanted to talk about it. Why didn't you celebrate Christmas before?"

"It's not important."

"Yes, it is."

"Listen what is it with you? I said it's not important. Now leave it alone. I don't know where you coming from sometimes. Sometimes you act like you a reporter, then the other times you acting like a therapist. What's up with that?"

"I'm sorry, Storm. I didn't mean to upset you. I just thought you might need to talk about it."

"Say that again."

"What?"

"Say the part after upset me. Say that part again."

"What? When I said I thought you might need to talk about it."

"Yeah."

"Why?"

"When you said that your voice sounded familiar to me. Lisa, tell me about you?"

"What? What do you need to know?"

"Well, tell me anything. All I know is that you are from Richmond, Virginia and that you are working on this documentary. If it wasn't for Taj assuring me that we could trust you, honestly speaking, I wouldn't even have you sitting here."

"I don't have a problem telling you about me. Where do you want me to start? What would you like to know?"

"Start at the beginning. Do you have any kids? That kind of stuff."

"First off, I should say I'm not from Richmond. I ended up in Richmond, by way of Brooklyn. I'm a New Yorker. And yes, I have one daughter and I had one son…but he died when he was two-years old."

"I'm sorry. How did he die?"

"He died of HIV complications."

"HIV? How did your baby catch HIV?"

"Through me."

"Oh, I'm sorry." *Maybe I should have left it alone.*

"I'm fine, Storm. Really, I am. But I wasn't always like this. I went through a lot to get where I am."

"Where are you?"

"I'm at peace with the things that I have done in the past. I've hurt a lot of people and because of that for years, I wanted to die. I tried killing myself eight times. No matter what I did, God didn't let me die."

"God?"

"Yes, God had a purpose for me."

"Listen, I told you before. That's your belief and everything I can respect that but don't come in talking about God to me. I don't wanna hear that crap?"

"I understand your pain, Storm. But you have to make peace with God."

"I don't have to do anything. Were you always glorifying God? Were you singing His praises when He took your innocent baby away from you?"

"No, I wasn't."

"How did I know that? So don't tell me about what I should do. You can't possibly know what I have been through."

"I can hear your pain each time you speak. You try hard to hide it but you can't hide it."

"Didn't I say I didn't wanna talk about me anymore? Why the fuck do you keep pushing the issue? Just leave me alone!"

"Alright. I'll leave you alone."

"I mean why can't we just stay on the subject. I thought you were talking about your life. Not mine. How did you get HIV?"

"I'm not sure. I was an addict. I started smoking-- snorting cocaine, then smoking crack, then shooting. I did a lot of things to maintain my habit. I'm embarrassed to say this, but I slept with many many men. And I slept with many women. Who knows when or how I contracted it."

"I can't believe you used to do that? I can't see you. But you seem like you have it so together. You seem like you always had it together. What changed for you? What made you change your life around?"

"Well, I was in this bad relationship. I mean I was always in one bad relationship after the other, but this one was terrible. One night, Pooch—that was his name--came home and just started fighting me. He woke me up whipping my behind. We fought and fought. Until this day, I still don't remember what he accused me of doing. But he whipped my behind until I staggered out of the apartment into the middle of the street. Some woman came by and saw me laying in the gutter and called the paramedics.

"The paramedics took me to Chippenham Hospital. In the emergency room, there was a domestic violence advocate there at the time. Her name was Tonya Blount. Tonya was a survivor of domestic violence and had become an advocate for women and children. That night, she was there picking up another battered woman to take to the shelter that she owned. Something or should I say Divine intervention sent her to room number four. When I meant her, she shared her story with me and listening to her and the other woman that was assisting her…listening to their testimonies made me want another chance.

"I was tired. I was tired of running. I was tired of trying to kill myself only to wake up the next morning. I had hurt so many people. Especially my kids…especially my daughter. No matter how much I drugged myself up, or how much I drank, I couldn't escape the pain. There was no escaping the pain."

"So, what happened? Where is your daughter now?"

"Well, my daughter is doing fine now. She's happy. She's in love and she unfortunately had to take care of herself and nothing I ever do can fix or undo what has been done already."

"You moved in with the lady, Tonya?"

"No, I moved into a shelter that she owned. Every Sunday a driver from the church would come and pick up the women who wanted to go to church. Every Sunday, I stayed behind."

"Why?"

"I was angry with God."

"Not you?"

"Yes, me. But I knew deep down inside that the devil was just keeping me from Him. The longer I stayed away from God and the longer I stayed angry, would be the longer I would be in bondage. Nobody could tell me how to get there. Yes, many people tried. Many people told me I couldn't walk around living the way I was. But I had to remove the roadblocks myself. I had to let God in."

"When did the change come for you?"

"Well, it was on my daughter's birthday. I never forget. I always suffered from depression. Around holidays, and birthdays it was always worse for me. Everything—all my pain, all my problems seem to magnify. One of the women told Tonya it was my daughter's birthday and they all threw her a birthday party. That day I made a wish that I would honor my daughter and my son's memory by living everyday to the fullest and I would no longer try and take the life that I didn't give myself...that didn't belong for me to take."

"I don't understand why you couldn't celebrate your daughter's birthday though. Who had her?"

"A close friend of mine and she moved a lot so I always had a hard time finding her."

"What's your daughter's name?"

I heard footsteps and I smelled the scent of Taj's cologne. I smiled, he was back.

"Hey, there. Everything okay?"

"Yes. You are back so fast."

"I know. I got outside and starting wandering around. I walked to one corner and I would forgot where I was going. Then I walked to the other corner and I forget where I needed to go, so I came back here. I couldn't focus outside. I guess I didn't want to leave my baby."

"Taj, you gotta leave me sometime. You gotta take care of your business. We can't have everything falling apart. We gonna need to eat you know when this is all over. I mean the hospital bills have already probably stopped us from buying that mansion."

"Ain't nothing gonna stop me from buying you that mansion. Don't you worry...we good."

"The doctor never came," Lisa said.

"He didn't? Let me go and curse out these damn nurses."

"Calm down, Taj. I think it's going down. Come and feel me."

Taj put his hand on my forehead, then on my neck. "I think you right. I think it has gone down some. Still though, they needed to be on their job and they ain't on the job. I'll be back."

As Taj walked out of the room, Lisa said, "You got a good man there. I'm happy for you."

"Thank you. I couldn't have made it this far without him. I don't know why, but he stands by me—no matter what."

"You don't know why? You have to ask? You are beautiful, Storm?"

"Correction, I *was* beautiful."

"You still are—inside and out."

Taj came back in with a nurse. "Here baby, open your mouth. I got you some Tylenol."

The nurse then checked my temperature. "It's gone down a little bit."

"When is the doctor gonna get here? I'm mean what kind of shit is this?"

"I just spoke with him. He'll be here in about a half hour."

"Well, I guess I'll be going," Lisa said.

"Oh, listen, Lisa, thanks for stopping by."

"Taj, no need to thank me. It was certainly my pleasure."

"Thanks, Lisa. When did you say you were leaving for Richmond again?"

"Uh, I don't know exactly. I'll be back tomorrow. Is that okay?

"Yeah, that's fine."

After Lisa left, the doctor came in. Taj and the doctor went out in the hallway corridor and spoke. Despite the whispering, I could hear the doctor tell Taj that I had another infection.

"What did the doctor say?"

"Nothing. You doing a lot betta."

"Stop lying, Taj."

"I'm not."

"Yes, you are, too. And you don't have to speak to the doctor outside in the hallway every time he comes here. I'm a big girl. I can handle whatever is going on with me. You know I don't like being kept in the dark."

"You just got another infection, Storm. That's all. They gonna start you on some antibiotics again and you'll be fine."

"I'm tired, Taj. I'm tired of this!"

"I know you are, Storm. I know this is a lot for you. But you have come a long way. Look at where you started at."

"I'm tired of hearing that story. Why can't I just get completely betta and go home."

"You will, soon."

The phone rang. It was Black.

"You wanna speak to him?"

"No. Tell him I will talk to him later."

"Yo, she falling asleep right now. I'll dial your number when she wakes up and let you talk to her."

"What he say?"

"He sound sad. I mean why don't you like talking to Black? He always been in your corner."

"Black reminds me why I'm here."

"He ain't have nothing to do with what Pam did."

"I know that. But that whole thing. I just don't wanna talk about it, Taj."

"Okay, baby. I'm not gonna force you to talk about it. When you ready. When you ready...we will talk about everything."

"How's Madison?"

"She's fine. My moms said she ate good today...she ate two steaks, and two pieces of fried chicken."

"Tell you mother she betta stop feeding my dog like that...she ain't gonna ever wanna come home."

I fell asleep and when I woke up, I heard Taj on his phone. I heard him giving commands in a whisper, "Knock 'em both off. Right now. Don't call me back until the shit is done."

"Taj what's going on? What are you talking about?"

"Nothing baby. Just taking care of some club business."

"Club business?"

"Yeah."

"Taj, you lying to me again. I don't like this. You know I don't like it when you lie to me. Stop that shit."

"Why can't you just take care of yourself? Focus on getting betta so we can start on the life we planned. Do that for me and let me do the worrying."

"What two are you talking about? The chicks that were with Pam?"

"Storm."

"Tell me!"

"Yeah and don't ask me nothing else 'cause I'm not gonna tell you nothing else." Taj tried to change the subject. "Valentine's day is right around the corner. What you want me to buy you?"

"Some new eyes."

"You have beautiful eyes."

"Eyes that I can't see out of."

"You know if I could do something about that I would. You know if I can make this all betta I would. You know that don't you?"

"Yes, I know that."

"Well, are you gonna tell me what you want?"

"I want to go home."

"Ma, you know I can't promise that."

"Why can't you?"

"We don't know if you gonna be okay to go home in another two weeks."

"If I'm not betta, I wanna go home anyway. We can hire a round the clock nurse, doctor and whatever else. Please Taj, I just wanna go home. I need to leave here. I feel like this room is sucking me in."

"Okay. I'll see what I can do."

Taj climbed into the bed with me and wrapped me up in his arms. "What do you want?" I asked.

"What?"

"What do you want for Valentine's Day?"

"I want Storm to be free."

Over the next few days, I had suffered a relapse. My daily visits from Rick, Taj's mother, and Lisa had increased. Taj had stopped leaving me again.

Lisa and I had grown close. Somehow, she had managed to earn and keep my trust. I shared with her my story—everything--from the beginning. When I cried, she cried. Sometimes, she was inconsolable.

"Storm, I'm gonna run out. I gotta take care of a few things."

"Okay, I'll be fine."

"You sure?"

"Yes," I said in a whisper.

"You know what? I'm not gonna leave today. I don't like the way you said that."

"What are you talking about, Taj?"

"You sound like you don't want me to leave."

"Taj, if I didn't want you to leave I would just say that. You know that."

"You sure you don't mind?"

"I'm positive."

"Okay."

"You didn't kiss me goodbye."

"I'm not leaving yet. I'm waiting for Lisa to get here."

"Oh, she's coming today?"

"Uh, uh. She should be here in a few minutes. And you know we never say goodbye. What's up with that?"

"Oh, I said goodbye?"

"Yeah."

"I didn't even realize I said that."

"You want me to turn on the television?"

"Yeah. Is cartoons still on?"

"Yeah, it's just nine o'clock. Actually its five minutes after nine."

"Oh, *Jimmy Neutron* is on."

"Yeah." Taj laughed. "He's on."

"Taj?"

"Yeah, Storm."

"I'm ready to go home."

"Okay, Storm. I know if you not out by next week, I'm gonna take you home."

"I'm ready to go home now."

"Storm, you too weak to go home now."

"I'll get stronger if you take me home."

"Storm, I have to make arrangements. I just can't walk out here with you like this. The hospital is not gonna let me discharge you out in the condition you are in today."

I started to cry.

"Why you crying, Storm?"

"I wanna go home."

"I know Storm. I promise you, just as soon as you get stronger, I'm gonna take you home."

"This isn't fair. This isn't fair. Why is this happening to me? Why do I have to go through this?"

Taj walked over to my bedside and lifted my head and embraced me. "I know, baby. I ask the same question everyday and I don't have an answer. I don't have an answer. All I know is it gotta get betta. It just gotta. I wish it were me laying here like this. I wish that it were me."

I touched Taj's hands. "You need a manicure."

Taj laughed. "You do, too."

"I need a makeover."

"No, you don't. You fine just as you are."

"I wanna dance, Taj."

"Okay. We gonna dance for Valentine's Day. I'm gonna buy you a fly ass red dress and I'm gonna buy me a Armani tux and we gonna dance. You know what, why don't we get married on Valentine's day?"

"Married?"

"Taj, I don't want to get married looking like this. In this condition."

"Why not? Why wait?"

"Are you sure?"

"Yeah, I'm sure."

"You don't wanna wait. I'm gonna get betta, Taj."

"No, I know that you are gonna get betta, but I don't wanna wait."

"Okay. Where?"

"I don't know. I'll figure that out."

"Taj, what about the yacht?"

"That's what's up. I didn't think of that. We will do it on the yacht."

"No matter what."

"No matter what."

"Taj, I still wanna dance?"

"Right now?"

"Uh-huh?"

"You shouldn't get out of bed, Storm. You are too weak."

"Please. I wanna do this."

"Okay." Taj walked over to the radio and turned it on. *Bonnie & Clyde* was playing. Taj immediately began to skip that CD.

"No, turn back. I wanna dance off of that."

"Storm, we play that all the time. Besides, that's too fast."

"I wanna dance off of that Taj," I insisted.

Taj went back that track. Then he walked over and lifted me out of the bed.

I was too weak to stand, so instead he cradled me. Taj began to sing along with the song. "…in this life of sin, is me and my girlfriend."

"Thank you for coming into my life, Taj."

"No, thank you for coming *into* my life."

"I love you, Taj."

"I love you more, Storm."

* * *

After Taj and I danced, Lisa came. "How are you today, Storm?"

"I'm okay."

"I heard you had a rough night."

"I did. But I'm betta."

"Why are smiling?"

"Because Taj and I danced today?"

"You did?"

"Yes."

"That's wonderful."

"Lisa, I love him."

"I know that you do, Storm. You know who I met today?"

"Who?"

"Madison."

"You did? Isn't she beautiful?"

"Yeah. She's very friendly."

"Where did you see here at?"

"Rick has her downstairs. I think he was waiting for Taj to come and get her."

"Oh, that's good. She hasn't been up here in a while."

"Oh, before I forget. Here my friend, Tonya gave me this to give to you."

"It feels like a CD."

"It is. Would you like for me to open it?"

"Yes. Who is it?"

"Helen Baylor?"

"Helen Baylor? Who is that?"

"She a gospel artist. I'm sorry. Tonya doesn't know."

"It's fine. Put it on."

"You want me to play the CD?"

"Yes. It's fine, Lisa."

Lisa walked to the radio and placed the CD in it. "Would you mind listening to my favorite song?"

"Go ahead. You listen to this music, too?"

"This music is what inspired me to keep going."

Then I heard this woman singing. She had a beautiful voice. "My God is an Awesome God," she sang.

When the song was done, I asked Lisa to turn off the radio.

"Lisa?"

"Yes, Storm?"

"Could you come here, please?"

"Sure."

Lisa walked over to my bedside. I reached for her hand. It was her left hand. Then I reached for her right hand. On her right hand there was a scar. A thick scar, shaped like a lobster. One that I was familiar with, one I would never forget. I traced the scar and then I heard Lisa sniffling.

"Lisa?"

"Yes, Storm?"

"Do you think God would hear me if I spoke to Him right now?"

"Of course, Storm. God will hear you. Speak to Him, Storm. It's alright baby. Speak to Him."

"God, I'm sorry. I'm sorry God. Please forgive me. And God if you hear me, could you please send my Momma."

"Storm?"

"Yes?"

"I am your Momma."

I turned my head, and a single tear rolled down my cheek. My breathing became shallow once again. Then I heard voices, I heard Miss LT. I smiled and then I closed my eyes.

Epilogue

On Valentine's Day, Taj, his mother Lisa, Rick, Black, Rosa, Lisa's pastor Bishop Long and her friend, Tonya flew to the Hamptons. At three o'clock in the evening they all boarded Taj's yacht – *Perfect Storm*. They ate Storm's favorite food, laughed, reminisced and traded their most memorable memories of Storm.

As the sun began to set, Rick stood up and solemnly stared into the sea. Then he sung, *Amazing Grace*. Taj asked everyone to gather around. Bishop Long led them in prayer. Taj cradled the Urn carrying Storm's ashes.

Finally, Taj grabbed Lisa's hand and they walked over to the railing and together they removed the lid and poured Storm's ashes into the sea in which she loved.

About the Author

TONYA BLOUNT is also the author of *Leaving the Wilderness,* and *Jay's Mansion.*

Tonya was born and raised in Brooklyn, New York. She presently divides her time between Long Island, New York and a suburb outside of Richmond, Virginia.

You may contact her at tonyablount@yahoo.com. You can also visit the author online at www.TonyaBlount.net

Other Titles by
Two of A Kind Publishing

Swingers

by Torrian Ferguson

Little Ghetto Girl

by Danielle Santiago

Cha-Ching

by Tonya Blount

To order visit

www.twoofakindpublishing.com

Attention Writers

Two of a Kind Publishing is currently seeking new authors of urban fiction including poetry, testimonies and autobiographies.

Submission Guidelines

- Synopsis and first four chapters required
- Typed, double-space, 1 ½ inch margins all around and only on one side of the page
- 12-point font in Times New Roman
- Cover letter stating address, phone number, the type of work being submitted
- A photo of author

No manuscripts will be returned. Please include a self-addressed, stamped envelope for a prompt response.

All manuscripts should be addressed to:

Two of a Kind Publishing
Attn: Submissions
3120 Milton Road Ste
Charlotte, NC 28215

Check us out on the web for information on our latest publications and featured authors at www.twoofakindpublishing.com